What had he done

Matthew watched from ~~~ out of her car, stretching ~~~ shaking her hair out of her eyes. ~~~ and cross, he thought, and incredibly beautiful.

Damn. If those jeans fitted her any tighter they'd cut off her circulation. She opened the boot of her car and bent over, treating him to an inviting curve of taut bottom.

He groaned and dropped his forehead against the glass. She was going to drive him crazy...

Caroline Anderson's nursing career was brought to an abrupt halt by a back injury, but her interest in medical things led her to work first as a medical secretary, and then, after completing her teacher training, as a lecturer in Medical Office Practice to trainee medical secretaries. She lives in rural Suffolk with her husband, two daughters, mother and assorted animals.

THE
REAL FANTASY

BY
CAROLINE ANDERSON

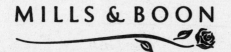

MILLS & BOON

MILLS & BOON, the Rose Device and
LOVE ON CALL are trademarks of the publisher.
Harlequin Mills & Boon Limited,
Eton House, 18-24 Paradise Road, Richmond, Surrey TW9 1SR

© Caroline Anderson 1996

ISBN 0 263 79854 2

Set in Times 10 on 11^1/$_2$ pt. by
Rowland Phototypesetting Limited
Bury St Edmunds, Suffolk

03-9610-47277

Made and printed in Great Britain

PROLOGUE

'How about this? "Busy general practice in bustling seaside town close to Lymington offers year's post to trainee"—blah, blah—"ten minutes from the beautiful countryside of the New Forest" et cetera, et cetera.' Tricia brandished her toast at the view through the window of the concrete tower block opposite. 'Beats this dump. Why don't you apply?'

'Lymington?' Linsey wrinkled her nose and scraped her long blonde hair back from her face. 'Funny things happened to me in Lymington. I'm not sure I want to go back—it wasn't my lucky place, really.'

Tricia's delicately pretty face screwed up with remorse. 'Oh, Lord, yes, you nearly drowned. Sorry. Forget it.'

'I fell off a boat into about five feet of water,' Linsey said drily. She leant back in the chair, arms raised above her head, and twisted her hair into a knot at her nape. Murky, weedy water, covering thick, clinging mud that had nearly claimed her life. If he hadn't been there—

She released her hair and it fell, slithering down her back like golden rain. 'It was no big deal,' she lied.

Tricia eyed her sceptically. 'If you say so. Still, you've got to train somewhere and it sounds nice. Why don't you apply? Perhaps you'll meet your mystery doctor again,' Tricia teased gently.

Linsey's mouth lifted at one corner in a reluctant smile. 'Unlikely. He wouldn't still be there—not after eight years.'

5

Tricia sank neat, even teeth into her toast and looked across at her friend. 'Why not?' she mumbled.

Linsey shrugged. There was no reason—no reason at all. Lots of doctors built up their practices in one place and stayed there for the whole of their professional lives. There was no reason at all to suppose that her mystery rescuer would be any different. The thought had a certain appeal. . .

Linsey's nose wrinkled again, but she reached across the breakfast table and plucked the professional journal out of her flatmate's hand. 'Where's the ad?'

The toast waved again. 'There—middle of the page.'

She turned her eyes to the advert. Tricia was right. The New Forest, with or without her mystery doctor, had to be better than the outskirts of Birmingham, especially for her with her love of the sea.

There were days, working here in this landlocked community, when she thought she'd die for want of the screaming of the gulls and the tug of the salt wind in her hair. She hardly ever sailed any more, but she loved to. Perhaps she'd have a chance, if she got the job.

She slid back her chair, then, scooping up the journal in one hand, she wandered out of the kitchen into the sitting room and curled up on the saggy old sofa, her long legs tucked up, bare feet under her bottom. Tricia followed her, plopping down beside her on the ancient sofa, her diminutive figure hardly denting it.

Delicate, almost fragile beauty as she was, Tricia had all the tenacity of a pit bull terrier. 'Going to apply?' she persisted.

Linsey shrugged again. 'I might.' She glanced at the date on the magazine, then at her watch. Today's, and if she moved fast she might get the letter in the post before she had to be at the hospital. She was on duty this weekend and if she didn't apply now she'd miss the boat. She had a copy of her CV and a letter of application ready in her computer. All she had to do was add the specifics of the job, juggle the wording a little to suit the occasion, print it and bung it in the post. 'Yes, I think I will.'

It took ten minutes. They drove to the postbox in Linsey's car because it was the only one with petrol in it, posted the letter of application and went on to the hospital, arriving in the nick of time.

They parted in the car park, Tricia for Obstetrics and Gynaecology, Linsey for Accident and Emergency. As she walked in, an ambulance screamed up to the entrance and within seconds the trolley was bowling through the doors, a paramedic working furiously to resuscitate someone while another ambulanceman ran alongside with a breathing bag.

'Catch,' Linsey said to the receptionist, threw her coat and her tote bag and followed the trolley down the corridor to Resus at a run. 'I'll take over,' she told the paramedic, and her hands slid over his, picking up the rhythm immediately.

'Intubate, please. Let's get some monitor leads on here fast as well.' She turned to the paramedic. 'Right, do we have any history?'

Flung head first into the grim reality of life and death, Linsey didn't give Lymington, her mystery doctor or the letter another thought.

'This one sounds good.'

Matthew Jarvis ran his eye over the profferred application letter, scanned the CV and frowned.

'What now?' Rhys growled.

He shrugged evasively. 'I'm not sure we want a woman.'

The big man sprawled across the sofa sighed with exasperation and stabbed his hand through tousled black hair, not for the first time. It had already suffered considerably throughout the sifting process they were engaged in.

'Matthew, we need a woman,' he said patiently. 'With Rosie retiring, we have to replace her with a woman. If we get a sufficiently good trainee, we could take her on. We've agreed that. Most of the others we've pulled out have been women. Why pick on this one to turn into a misogynist?'

Matthew grinned involuntarily and glanced down, a frown gathering on his forehead again. It was the name of the applicant that put him off, but he could hardly tell Rhys that without sounding like a totally off-the-wall nut case. He made himself read the letter again, and finally set it down on the miserably deficient 'maybe' pile. They really didn't have a great deal to choose from, he admitted wearily to himself, and hers was the last letter—and the best.

'OK, we could look at her,' he conceded.

Rhys unravelled his legs and stood up. 'Thank God for that. Right, I'm going home, such as it is. I'll see you tomorrow. We'll go over them all again and draw up an interview list from that bewildering selection.' His mouth tilted in a wry smile and, with a waggle of his fingers, he left.

'Such as it is'. Matthew watched through the window of the little sitting room at the back of the practice as his friend and colleague went out to his car, started it up and drove off. Was his home life falling apart still? Rhys and his wife had had a rough patch before the third baby had come along. Matthew didn't suppose another batch of sleepless nights and postnatal depression was helping either of them. He made a mental note to pay Judy a social call one day, just to check up on her. He turned back to the table and picked up the top letter again.

Linsey Wheeler. Unusual spelling. It was that, of course, that had set off alarm bells.

The only other Linsey he had known had had a catastrophic effect on his life, quite literally. One chance encounter had changed the course of history for ever.

A twinge of guilt and remorse plucked at him yet again, but he suppressed it. He had to move on.

And that reminded him. . .

He reached for the phone, jabbed in a number and leant back in the chair, the letter still in his hand. 'Jan— I'm sorry. I've been held up at the surgery.'

The voice at the other end was resigned. 'That's OK, Matthew. I understand.'

He felt another twinge of guilt and remorse, this one from a different source and touched with irritation. If only she'd yell at him, rant a bit, act as if she cared.

But he didn't want her to, of course. What he wanted was her indifference, so that his own went unnoticed.

His conscience prickling, he arranged to ring her in a few days, then hung up the receiver and turned his attention back to the letter.

Linsey.

His eyes lost focus, gazing far into the past—so far that fact and fantasy had blurred at the edges.

She had had beautiful hair. That had been the first thing he'd noticed about her. He hadn't been able to take his eyes off it. Long, golden, falling around her shoulders like a glossy curtain, slithering over one arm as she turned her head and met his eyes.

Green eyes. Jade-green, the colour of a tropical sea, crystal-clear and pure, not the murky, greasy sea he had plucked her from just moments later—the sea that had nearly claimed her life.

A shudder ran through him. If he hadn't been there, she might have died.

And Sara would be his wife.

CHAPTER ONE

LINSEY felt marvellous. The sun was shining, the gulls were screaming overhead and the salt-laden wind was tugging at her hair. Standing on the waterfront near the Royal Lymington Yacht Club, listening to the gulls and the rhythmic slap of the rigging against the masts as the boats rocked at their moorings, she felt as if she'd come home.

She looked over to the right, to the place where she had nearly drowned, and felt nothing. Good. She had been worried that it might unsettle her, but it didn't. It had all been over so quickly—all except the image of those astonishing gun-metal-grey eyes, the colour of a stormy sea.

She could still see his eyes as he'd bent over her, smoothing her hair back from her face, the gesture unexpectedly tender.

'Who are you?' she'd asked, her voice croaky and hoarse with the swallowed water, and he'd smiled like quicksilver.

'My name's Matthew. I'm a doctor. You're all right now; just rest for a moment. They've called an ambulance.'

'Stay with me,' she'd begged, hanging on his arm, and so he had, his fingers laced with hers, his other hand smoothing her hair rhythmically. His voice had been deep and soothing—a reassuring murmur that gradually replaced the thunder of her heartbeat as it steadied.

Then the ambulance had come and whisked her away,

but the look in his eyes had stayed with her, warming her chilled body and dissolving her fear.

He had visited her that evening, just briefly, bringing her flowers and refusing to stay.

'My fiancée's waiting,' he'd said, and she'd felt a crazy and irrational disappointment.

The following morning her parents had taken her home from the hospital, none the worse for her ordeal and only slightly sorry to miss the end of her sailing holiday.

She had never seen him or heard from him again, but she had never forgotten him, or what he had done for her.

She turned now and headed back towards her car, parked nearby in one of the quiet streets. Her interview was in half an hour, and she had to find the practice yet.

She followed the signs through Lower Pennington to Milhaven, and then turned down a quiet, leafy road off the high street. About halfway along, amongst the dentists and the orthodontists and the premises of other GPs, she found the surgery.

'Drs Jarvis, Farmer, Williams and Wilson', it said on a shiny brass plate on the gatepost. A big, double-fronted Edwardian semi-detached house with tile-hung elevations, it was welcoming and friendly, with colourful hanging baskets and pots by the front door to welcome patients. There was parking for them in what had been the front garden, and a sign pointing round the back said, 'Parking For Surgery Staff Only. Please Keep Clear.'

According to the letter in Linsey's bag, there were three men and one woman in the practice, with two nurses, a practice manager, two receptionists and a part-time accountant as well as the district nurses and midwives, chiropodist, dietician and physiotherapists attached to the practice, and the trainer was Dr J M Jarvis.

She eyed the parking space at the front, then the sign pointing to the back. The surgery was obviously still busy, judging by the number of patients' cars. She drove down the back, parked in the space labelled 'Visitor' and headed towards the front door.

As she did so a head appeared at one of the windows on the ground floor in what looked like a little extension. 'Dr Wheeler?'

She stopped. 'Yes?'

The face smiled. 'Come on in through the back door. It's open.'

She did as instructed and was greeted by the smiling face, this time attached to a plump, maternal body.

Her hand was warmly shaken. 'I'm Suzanne White, the practice manager. Come on in. The doctors are still busy in surgery at the moment, I'm afraid, but they'll be with us soon. Can I get you a cup of coffee while we wait for them?'

'Oh, please. That would be lovely after my journey.'

She followed the short, plump woman through into the kitchen. 'Have a seat, Dr Wheeler,' Suzanne suggested, and Linsey made herself at home at the kitchen table. The coffee was real, from a filter machine, and smelled wonderful. Suzanne set two mugs on the table and pulled out the chair opposite; then, seated, her dumpy hands wrapped round her own mug, she chatted cheerfully.

'Find us all right? It's quite easy.'

'Yes, no problems. The directions were excellent.' She had guessed that the directions were from Suzanne, and, judging by the slight warmth in the woman's face, Linsey thought she was right. Well, it wouldn't hurt to be on the right side of the practice manager, she reasoned, quelling the little wriggle of guilt.

'It gets a bit easier as the season comes to an end. The tourist traffic can make it all a bit confusing. Summer is usually the worst, of course. Do you know the area?'

'Only slightly. I had a sailing holiday here once, years ago.'

'Ah, a nautical type. Do you still sail?'

Linsey shook her head and smiled. 'No. I haven't had much chance in Birmingham. I'd like to start again, though, and I love to be near the sea.'

'Oh, so do I. I can't go on it, mind—I get as sick as a parrot just thinking about it; but there's something about the atmosphere—nothing else is quite like it, and nothing can take its place for me, summer or winter.' She sat back, her smile warm and relaxed. 'So, when did you decide you wanted to be a GP?'

Linsey sensed she was being interviewed now, but it didn't matter. The answer to this question was easy.

'Eight years ago—down here, actually. I met a doctor under rather fortuitous circumstances.' She gave a little laugh. Talk about understatement. 'Anyway, I was eighteen, I didn't know what I wanted to do with my life and because there's nobody medical in my family it just hadn't occurred to me. It did then, though, and I realised it was the least I could do.'

Suzanne's brow creased. 'The least you could do? In what way?'

Linsey shrugged slightly. 'I owed him my life, quite literally, and training as a doctor was the only way I could think off to repay the debt—put something back in humanity's pot, if you like. It all sounds a bit melodramatic and crazy, doesn't it, really? But at the time it seemed quite logical!'

Suzanne laughed. 'I'm sure it was, and it's as good a reason as any for going in for medicine. I'm sure a lot of people have weaker reasons.'

'I'm sure too,' Linsey agreed, thinking of some of the people she had trained with. 'Anyway, that was what I ended up doing, and thank God I did, because I discovered that I love medicine and I can't imagine doing anything else. I just wish I could thank him. I owe him more than I can ever say. I really didn't want to drown!'

'Drown?' Suzanne's eyes widened. 'I thought he'd detected some insidious disease or something!'

'Oh, no.' Linsey laughed. 'I haven't had a day's illness in my life—well, apart from breaking my leg as a child. No, he pulled me out of the river.'

'The river?' Suzanne's eyes widened even further. 'Good gracious. Tell me more about this rescue. It all sounds terribly dramatic.'

Linsey laughed softly. 'It was, for a few short seconds. I'd had a bit to drink and I fell off a boat. He fished me out of the river at Lymington.'

'I see what you mean about fortuitous! He really did save your life.'

'Oh, yes. I wasn't joking. I suppose any good swimmer could have got me out of the water and any first-aider could have revived me, and there were plenty of people there, so if it hadn't been him it would have been someone else. That's not the point, though. He made me think about medicine as a career, and it's the best thing that's ever happened to me.'

A snort behind her made her turn, and she looked up—and up—at a tall man with dark hair and laughing grey eyes. 'Clearly you've not been in medicine long enough. Still, you're just starting. Perhaps in a few years you'll be jaded like the rest of us. I take it you're Dr

Wheeler? I'm Rhys Williams. The others will be along in a tick, I expect, barring earthquake and civil commotion.'

She smiled and shook the profferred hand, liking the big, friendly man immediately, and Dr Williams hooked out a chair, reversed it and settled his large, solidly muscled body on it. His hands engulfed the steaming mug of coffee that Suzanne put in front of him, and he turned to Linsey again.

'So, you're a career doctor, are you?' he said with a grin. 'I wonder how long that'll last.'

She returned the grin. 'It's lasted so far. I see no reason why it should stop now.'

'Paperwork?' he said wryly.

She laughed. 'Every job has its downside. Look on the bright side—you could have been an accountant!'

Rhys shuddered eloquently. 'God forbid. I'll settle for endless form-filling. Ah, here's the boss.'

Still laughing, Linsey turned towards the door as another man entered, shrugging out of his sports jacket. As he did so a little shiver of awareness shimmered through her. Adrenalin, or another equally basic hormone? Both, probably.

Her eyes devoured him, taking in the lean, rangy build and powerful shoulders at a glance. He was big—not quite as tall or as solid as Rhys, but big for all that—his mid-brown hair cut conventionally short, his immaculate white shirt tapering from broad shoulders to tuck into well-cut khaki trousers that hugged his slim hips and emphasised the long, rangy legs.

She took all this in in the brief second before he met her eyes, and then without warning her heart jammed in her throat. Those eyes! It couldn't be. . .

'Matthew?' she said breathlessly.

His face was stunned for a moment, then warmth flared in his eyes—those incredible, dark gun-metal eyes that she had never forgotten.

He dropped his jacket over a chair and walked towards her as she stood up, reaching out for her hands. His fingers were warm and hard and strong—fingers that had plucked her from the jaws of death—and she clung to them as he stared at her. 'Linsey?' he said questioningly, his voice disbelieving. His eyes tracked her face, registering the eyes, the mouth, the hair. His knuckles brushed her cheek. 'My God, it really is you.'

She felt the silly grin but could do nothing to hide it. 'Yes, it is. It really is. This is amazing. Oh, Matthew— I've just been talking about you!' With a delighted laugh she flung her arms round him and hugged him hard.

After a brief hesitation his arms came up and hugged her back, then he held her at arm's length and looked at her for a moment, shaking his head slowly from side to side.

If the others hadn't been there she might have stayed there all day gazing into his eyes, but with the remnants of her presence of mind she straightened away from him and gave another little laugh.

'Wow, you look different to what I remember.'

'So do you—cleaner, for a start. And vertical. I hadn't realised you were so tall.'

She wrinkled her nose. 'Don't. Being five foot ten isn't exactly an advantage in life.'

'You can see over the crowds.'

She laughed. 'Especially at a party. Straight over the top of most of the men there.'

He looked down into her eyes. 'Not all of them.'

'No.' She returned his gaze, conscious of his height and nearness. 'No, not all of them.' She pulled herself together. 'Do you know, I've waited so long to thank you for what you did?'

He laughed awkwardly. 'You did thank me. Over and over again. So, I take it you were all right? No after-effects? Dreams—that sort of thing?'

Dreams? Oh, yes, there had been dreams—and he had starred in most of them. She could hardly tell him that, because it wasn't at all what he meant. She carefully schooled her expression. 'No. No after-effects.'

'Is this your phantom rescuer, then?' Suzanne asked curiously.

Linsey dragged her eyes from Matthew's and turned to the practice manager. 'Yes—yes, he is.' She gave a self-conscious laugh. 'My mystery doctor.'

'Hardly a mystery.' His voice was gruff, and as she looked up at him she saw that his eyes were bright with emotion. He moved away from her, clearing his throat, taking the coffee-mug Suzanne pushed into his hands.

'So,' he said at last, 'is this just coincidence that you're here?'

The silly grin was back. 'Yes. Absolutely. Well, not entirely, I suppose, in that I thought it would be appropriate to come back to where it all started, but I had no idea it was your practice.'

He looked confused, but Suzanne filled him in.

'It was here she decided to become a doctor, apparently, after you fished her out of the river.'

'Really? It's my fault?'

She nodded. 'Yes. So I hope you're going to finish what you started and offer to train me.' Her grin was irrepressible, and behind Matthew she saw Rhys snort with laughter.

'Oh, I think it would be obligatory, don't you, Matthew?'

Matthew's eyes cut to his colleague, one brow arched.
'I think it would be appropriate to find out first if we're
all able to offer what the other party wants, don't you?'

Oops. Linsey realised she'd overstepped the mark,
but she couldn't retract the words and she didn't want
to. Instead she added to them, softening the effect with
a teasing smile. 'Oh, of course. It's always possible that
I may not want to train here. After all, I hardly met you.
I might have imagined all those sterling qualities.'

Matthew blushed, to her amazement, and Rhys, far
from looking offended by Matthew's put-down, laughed
again. 'Very likely,' he said agreeably, and shot Linsey
a grin. 'How long ago was it?'

'Eight years.'

'Yes, it must be,' Matthew agreed. His colour was
back to normal but he was watching Linsey curiously.
'I'd just started here as a trainee myself. God, it feels
like a lifetime.' He pulled himself together visibly and
looked at Rhys. 'Rosie's on the drag and Tim's out on
a call. Shall we have some lunch while we wait?'

Rhys nodded. 'Sure. I'm starving; I missed breakfast
again. The others can join us when they're ready.'

'I've put it all out in the sun room,' Suzanne told
them, and then made herself scarce while Matthew led
them through into the room from which Suzanne had
waved to Linsey as she'd arrived. A small extension, it
overlooked the car park at the back, but it was warm
and sunny, there were tall trees to offer interest and it
was obviously their cherished retreat. She could imagine
them snoozing there between clinics after a busy night
on call, catnapping as only doctors seemed able to do.

A delicious cold buffet was set out on the low table
between the wicker chairs, and at Matthew's suggestion
she helped herself and then took one of the chairs,

sinking down into the soft, welcoming cushions. Oh, yes, definitely a place for snoozing and retreating—but not now.

Matthew sat opposite her, Rhys on the big sofa, his long legs stuck out, the plate balanced on his lap.

He looked totally relaxed—unlike Matthew who was watching Linsey as if she were a bug under a microscope.

'So, you decided to take up medicine after you met me, is that right?'

She nodded.

'Is that a good enough reason? It seems rather fanciful to me.'

She laughed a little uneasily, uncomfortable with the criticism. She knew that he was just examining her motives, but even so. . .

'Not really. I didn't know what I wanted from life. If the truth be told I was a spoilt brat and I hadn't really given my future a second's serious thought. It was all getting a bit urgent, though, because it was the end of August and I'd prevaricated for so long that I'd lost the place I was offered at Oxford and it was a case of finding somewhere else to take me.'

'So did you start the year after?'

'No—no, that year. I rang up a few colleges and chatted to a few people and got a place in London.'

'Just like that?' Matthew said in astonishment.

She shrugged diffidently. 'I fulfilled the entry requirements.'

'Somewhat,' Rhys said through a forkful of chicken and rice. 'Four A grades at A level and an Oxbridge entrance pass. I should think they were falling over themselves to have you.'

She felt warmth steal over her skin and played with her food for a moment. 'Not really. They were a bit sceptical of my motives too. I had to work my charm a bit at the interview.'

'You must have been very convincing,' Matthew said drily.

'Apparently,' she agreed, ignoring his tone. 'They took me and I worked very hard to give them no cause to regret their decision.'

Matthew looked slightly disbelieving. 'So, like Saul on the road to Damascus, the scales fell from your eyes and you saw the light, knuckled under and stopped playing at life, is that right?'

She was astonished. Why was he so hostile all of a sudden? Because she'd made that joke about him having to take her on? Oh, hell—her and her big mouth.

'Something like that,' she replied, trying to keep her tone light.

'So why general practice?'

'Variety? I'd get bored specialising in one field. I love people and their problems and difficulties. I suppose I'm an inveterate Nosy Parker, and I can't bear people coming and going in clinics without any continuity. I thought general practice would give me a chance to get to know families and work with them over a long period of time.'

'To satisfy your curiosity?'

Lord, she'd asked for it. She should never have said 'Nosy Parker'. When would she learn to think before she spoke? 'No, not to satisfy my curiosity,' she corrected him. 'More to give me an opportunity to do the job properly.'

'And is that important to you?'

'Yes, of course.'

'There's no ''of course'' about it. Lots of people end

up in general practice because they're no good at anything else.'

Her mouth tightened. 'Well, I'm sorry to disappoint you but I'm not one of them.' Her voice was serious now and she gave up on any attempt to charm him with light-hearted banter. Clearly it wasn't what he wanted to hear and he was determined to think the worst of her. He probably even thought she'd applied for the job knowing he was there, intending to trade on the tenuous link between them, and he had obviously decided— probably years ago—that she was a dumb blonde and a total airhead. She would have to prove him wrong.

She looked him in the eye and went on, 'If you believe general practice is for those who couldn't make it in hospital medicine then I don't think you should be a trainer.'

She heard a muffled snort of laughter from Rhys, and Matthew's eyebrows shot up. 'I wouldn't put it quite like that,' he said crisply. 'So, Dr Wheeler, would you like to elaborate on your theme of doing the job properly?'

She could hardly miss the splinter of sarcasm in his tone. She forced a smile. 'Of course. I think continuity of care is extremely important. Without it mistakes are made, people die needlessly and suffer unnecessarily because with the best will in the world we can't write down everything we observe, and the next doctor to see the patient hasn't got the necessary benchmarks.'

'Ah, but—we have to make sure they're provided,' Matthew insisted.

'But we can't, not always, not infallibly, because so much of it is instinct and intuition.'

'Instinct? Intuition?' he said sceptically.

'I agree,' Rhys said quietly. 'That's exactly why I'm

a GP, and why I—and you, Matthew, and Rosie and Tim—go the extra mile to make sure things are followed up and dealt with. I think Linsey's understanding of the job is actually very accurate.'

'We still need to make full notes,' Matthew insisted.

'Oh, for God's sake, man, that goes without saying.'

'I don't think so. I think it needs to be clearly understood.'

'I clearly understand it,' Linsey said quietly into the fraught silence.

Both men turned to look at her.

'I wouldn't dream of making incomplete notes on a consultation just because I expect to be doing the follow-up. I wouldn't rely on my own memory and I couldn't be sure that I would be the one seeing the patient. That wasn't what I was saying. I was just trying to explain why I feel I, personally, want to be in a position to follow patients up and supervise their care to the conclusion of their treatment.'

She held Matthew's eyes in a challenging stare, defying him to differ with her again or question her motivation, and as she did so she saw the dawning of surprise—and, heavens, respect?—in their gun-metal depths.

The phone rang then, breaking the silence that stretched between them, shattering the tension and enabling Linsey to drag her eyes away from Matthew at last.

'So, tell us all about your training so far,' Rhys said easily, helping himself to more of the cold, creamy chicken mixture and tucking into it with relish.

'From the beginning?'

'Seems a good place to start,' Matthew said drily.

She gave a forced little laugh but did as she was asked,

starting at the beginning with her applications to medical colleges at various universities, her acceptance by a London college, her training, her natural leanings, the areas she had enjoyed and the areas she found difficult, when she'd made her decision to be a GP rather than a hospital doctor, and the training she had undergone since making that decision.

'Have you got an obstetrics qualification?' Matthew asked, knowing full well she had, if he'd read her application form.

'Yes. I've done my MRCOG.'

They nodded. The qualification was useful in general practice, enabling them to offer home births, contraceptive advice and other facilities related to that area. A woman with obstetric qualifications was especially valuable. It was one of Linsey's most significant assets, and she knew it. Another asset was her time in Accident and Emergency, which had a lot in common with general practice in that you never knew what was coming through the door. As a way of keeping a doctor on his or her toes it was unsurpassed.

Matthew brought it up.

'You're in Accident and Emergency at the moment?'

She nodded. 'Yes, that's right. I'm just finishing.'

'How have you found it?'

'Fascinating.' She told them about her casualty work, and how she found it stimulating even though it was very stressful.

'General practice can be stressful,' Matthew warned. 'All that continuity has its disadvantages. There's the pain of following a family through tragedy and the remorseless march of time, propping up carers, dealing with terminal illness, miscarriage, infertility, childhood cancers—emotionally it can be very, very draining.'

'I know. I don't mind—I'm not looking for an easy option. I think it's more important to do something useful; you didn't save my life so I could sit around and waste it.'

Matthew's smile was wry and a little strained. 'I don't think our actions are as carefully considered as that. I saved your life—if I did—because in that split second it was the obvious thing to do. If I hadn't, someone else would have. It was no big deal.'

'No big deal'. Exactly the words she had used to Tricia; but it was far from the truth. For her, at least, it had been a very big deal indeed, and she didn't think it had had that little impact on Matthew, either. Linsey got the feeling that there was more than modesty behind his remark. He seemed uncomfortable with the subject, as if it made him uneasy for some unknown reason. Obviously he didn't like to play the hero. Her heart softened towards him and she felt a resurgence of the affection with which she had remembered him all these years.

She wondered what it would take for him to look at her again as he had on that day, before she'd fallen in the water, when she had caught his eye. It had almost felt as if there was something between them, some magical pull that drew them together.

She nearly laughed aloud at her silliness. She'd have to stop thinking like this if she got the job. Heavens, he'd done nothing really to attract her single-minded interest, and she could hardly hold him responsible for the silly and irrational behaviour of her heart.

Anyway, he'd been engaged eight years ago, so presumably he'd been married now for years.

She almost asked, the question on the tip of her tongue before she remembered herself and clamped her lips on the words. It was none of her business. She was looking for a job as a trainee GP, not a mistress or girlfriend. This was professional. She must remember that. Just because he'd saved her life it gave her no claim on him—and anyway, the way the interview had gone so far she didn't think she stood a snowflake's chance in hell of getting the job. The problem was that she said what she felt, without editing her words in her mind— and that was not always welcome or appropriate. No, if he didn't want to offer her the job it would be her own fault. It was hardly his that he apparently didn't have a sense of humour.

She looked up at them, suddenly aware of the pregnant silence. 'I'm sorry?'

Matthew was looking at her oddly. 'I said, if we offered you the post as trainee, when would you be free to start?'

She blinked. Offered the post? Was he. . .? 'Um—the first of August,' she said hastily. 'Or any time after that.'

'OK. Rhys, anything else you want to ask Linsey?'

Rhys shook his head. 'No, I don't think so. I think you've about covered it,' he said drily.

Matthew flicked him an irritated glance and stood up, shaking Linsey's hand as she followed suit. 'Right. Well, we'll be in touch. We both have to get on now—feel free to stay and finish your lunch. There's some coffee in the kitchen, I expect. I'm sorry the others didn't make it, but that's general practice for you. Sorry to abandon you.'

Linsey thought that Matthew looked anything but sorry as he hurried out of the door. If anything he was making a hasty getaway—the faster the better. Rhys looked after him, puzzlement reflected on his face, and then turned back to her with a sympathetic smile.

'Sorry about that. He obviously decided to test you under pressure.'

She laughed. 'Yes—and I leaked like an old gas main. Oh, well. There'll be other jobs.'

'I shouldn't panic. I thought you stood up to him rather well.'

'But is that what he's looking for?'

Rhys's mouth quirked in a smile. 'Who knows? We're interviewing again tomorrow, so you should get a letter by the end of the week. If it helps at all, you've got my vote.'

She summoned a smile. 'Thanks. I don't think I've got Matthew's.'

Rhys's brow creased again. 'I wouldn't say that. He's often preoccupied. Probably something to do with a patient—I shouldn't take it personally. I'd show you the flat, but I have to go. I've got several calls to make.'

'The flat?'

'Yes, there's a flat that goes with the job—over the surgery, upstairs. It's very pretty—bit atticky, but I suppose it's all part of the charm. If you crane your neck it's got a sea view.' He grinned. 'Suzanne will show you.' He unfolded himself from the sofa, shook her hand and left, closing the door softly behind him.

Linsey sagged back against the cushions and let out a sigh of relief. As interviews went, that had been appallingly difficult. Still, even though she hadn't got the job—and she was sure she hadn't—at least she'd seen Matthew again and had a chance to thank him.

He might want to dismiss the incident, but she had no illusions about what she owed him.

She remembered again the tug of the weed at her hair, the slimy feel of it clinging round her arms, dragging her under. She shuddered with the memory. Her dress had caught on a propeller—fortunately stationary—and trapped her further as she struggled with the weeds and the clinging mud around her ankles, and she could remember the terror, the sheer blind panic of knowing she was going to die in that cold, sinister water and that nothing could save her.

Then, just as she was sliding into oblivion, she had felt the firm grip of a pair of strong masculine hands wrenching her free, and the next moment there had been the blessed sun on her face and the tender caress of his hand across her brow.

She might have made light of it to Tricia, but she had been badly frightened, and Matthew had known that. Clearly, though, however pleased he might have been to see her again and make sure she was all right, he wasn't going to let their slight acquaintance influence him positively towards her. If anything, he was leaning the other way.

Or maybe she had carried a false image of him all these years? There was no reason, of course, why they should get on. They had exchanged perhaps two dozen words altogether both at the quayside and later when he had brought her flowers in hospital. She didn't know him. Perhaps he was just a miserable, cheerless individual. Whatever, she sensed that he didn't like her. Another fantasy in the dust, she thought wryly. So much for the gun-metal eyes of my dreams. Anyway, he was married.

She put her plate down, her appetite quite gone. She had hardly touched the delicious lunch, she realised, so busy had she been defending herself and answering questions. She didn't want it now. All she wanted was to get away, to get back to Birmingham and her work in A and E, and to find time to curl up with this week's journals and look for another trainee post.

Skegness or Great Yarmouth or Blackpool, perhaps, if she wanted the sea. One thing she was sure of—she wouldn't be offered the post by Matthew Jarvis.

He might have saved her life once, but quite clearly he had decided that his responsibility to her started and ended there. She would have to look elsewhere to further her career.

She went and found Suzanne White. 'I'm going now—thank you for the coffee and the lunch.'

'Oh, my dear, I haven't shown you the flat yet!'

Linsey smiled. 'That's all right. I haven't really got time to look at it,' she lied.

'Well, I hope I see you again, dear,' Suzanne said with a genuinely friendly smile. 'We could do with your sunny face to brighten the place up.'

Linsey found her eyes misting over. 'Yes. Well, thanks. I hope so too. Goodbye.'

She let herself out of the back door, ran to her car and was just getting in when Matthew came out of the door.

'Are you off?'

She stood up again. 'Yes. I've got a long drive.'

He walked up to her, his eyes somehow haunted. 'I'm sorry I was a bit hard on you in there.'

She shrugged. So was she, but what could she do about it? Nothing. And nor could he. He looked awkward, staring at his hands and then back at her, his eyes belying the careful expression on his face.

'I just wanted to say I'm glad I've seen you again and that everything's all right.'

'You too,' she said, dredging up the tiniest smile. 'Well, goodbye again. I hope you find your trainee.'

She slid behind the wheel, slammed the door and reversed out without looking at him again. She caught

sight of him in the mirror as she paused at the roadside—
watching her, a thoughtful expression on his face.

She pulled out onto the road with a little spurt of
gravel, and her idol disappeared in a cloud of dust.

How appropriate. What a suitable ending for a fantasy.
She blinked the mist from her eyes and headed for
home. . .

CHAPTER TWO

'I THINK Linsey's the best.'

Matthew scowled at Rhys. 'You've made that quite obvious.'

Rhys shrugged. 'I have to work with her too, you know—maybe for ever.'

Matthew snorted. 'I don't think so. She's an airhead.'

'A dumb blonde? I hardly think so. Look at her qualifications, then look at your own—or is that the problem?' Rhys's voice was dry.

Matthew shook his head. Ego wasn't one of his problems, and his own exam results had been perfectly respectable. It wasn't her brain that worried him. 'I know she's academically gifted. That doesn't mean a thing in medicine. She has to be clever enough to have got this far. I'm more interested in her dedication and commitment, her motivation, her staying power.'

Rhys sighed. 'Have you read her references?' he said pointedly. 'She is outstanding. Nobody has said anything about her that wasn't positively dripping with accolades. And I liked her.'

'Fine. You liked her, so I have to work with her?'

Matthew knew that he was being irrational, but he couldn't discuss his feelings about Linsey—and for her—with a colleague, or even a very good friend. Admittedly, what he had seen of her was at odds with his memory of her, but eight years ago she had been flighty, light-headed and thoroughly silly—and he'd been knocked off his perch by her like a lovesick parrot.

He wasn't looking for an encore.

'OK, then, who else?' Rhys said, leaning back in the chair and folding his arms across his massive chest. The neutral expression on his face didn't reach his eyes, which glittered with challenge.

Damn. There he had him. There was nobody else—at least, no one who on paper or otherwise stood up to Linsey. She had made her stand and defended it well, and he found himself reluctantly admiring her for it.

'You were a pig to her,' Rhys said softly.

'Yes, I know. I apologised.'

Rhys grunted, studying Matthew's face searchingly. 'What happened between you eight years ago?' he asked out of the blue.

Matthew felt hot colour flood the back of his neck. 'Nothing.'

'You fancied her.'

'She was eighteen.'

'And I'll bet she was stunning. That's the problem, isn't it? The sexy little minx got under your skin and you can't cope with it.'

'Rubbish.' Matthew shifted uncomfortably, even more conscious of the heat reddening his neck.

Rhys's smile was knowing. 'Take her on. Keep her for the year, and have an affair with her. I think it would do you good.'

'Jan might have something to say about that,' he reminded Rhys mildly.

The rude snort that followed that remark needed no elaboration. 'Go on, Matthew. Live a little. Give your hormones some exercise for once.'

'Don't you have a home to go to?' Matthew prodded.

Rhys's face lost its animation. 'A home? You mean that shell with three whining kids and a woman who doesn't want to know me? Yeah, I've got a home.'

Matthew leant forward and put his hand on his friend's big, bony knee. 'I'm here, old man, if you want to chat.'

'Thanks.' Rhys's voice was subdued, his face shuttered. 'I think I will go, actually. Emma was sick this morning and Judy won't be coping well. I'd better go and rescue them all from each other. I'll see you tomorrow.'

Matthew watched him go, and worried. Things seemed to go from bad to worse. He must see Judy—and he must make a decision on this trainee. If Rhys and Judy were heading for a crisis, perhaps it had better be someone who was free to start soon. Rosie didn't actually leave until October, but if he could get someone before then—perhaps at the beginning of August? It never hurt to have extra cover during the silly season. People seemed to wait until they were on holiday to become ill, for some reason, and their workload always doubled in the summer months.

Yes, someone who could start promptly could well be worth considering. There were only a couple, of course, the dreaded Linsey one of them.

Lord, she was lovely. Rhys was right, needless to say. She had got under his skin eight years ago. He'd only seen her twice—the first time when she'd fallen in, the second when he'd dropped into the hospital on his way to pick Sara up for the evening, just to make sure that the subject of his heroism was doing well.

That second visit had been a mistake. She'd looked at him with those enormous jade-green eyes and thanked him in a soft, slightly throaty voice that had become woven into his dreams over the next few weeks to the detriment of his sanity—and his relationship with Sara.

Still, he was older now, there was Jan to consider and on closer inspection Linsey was not the stuff of his fantasies. Instead she was quirky, opinionated and down-right cheeky. The meek, sweet, wide-eyed, fawning girl of his fantasies had been rudely supplanted by a robust, quick-witted woman who was nobody's fool.

On second thoughts, that made her even more exciting.

He tipped back his head and groaned. Why, oh, why had she come back into his life?

There was an easy answer, of course: don't give her the job. Offer it to someone else.

And miss the chance of a lifetime?

He swore softly. The chance for what? He was committed to Jan—had been tiptoeing round the issue of marriage for months. He had no doubt that, if he'd been pushed, he would have been sleeping with her, but she'd seemed happy to let it drift, and he'd been so busy at work over the summer that there honestly hadn't been any opportunities.

Perhaps it was time to push ahead on that front, and forget about aggravating blondes with attitude. He'd find someone else for the job.

He shuffled the letters and interview notes endlessly, but came up with the same answer every time. What he didn't know was why. . .

'You've got it! You've got the job! Oh, Linsey!'

Tricia hugged her stunned friend, snatched the letter out of her hand and read it aloud.

'"Dear Dr Wheeler, thank you for attending your recent interview. We should like to offer you the post of registrar in general practice with us—salary as per scale attached, training hours by arrangement to suit schedules", blah blah, et cetera.' She dropped the letter on the coffee-table and plopped down beside Linsey on the sofa. 'The first of August? That's next week! Talk about leaving it till the last minute! You'll have to pack up and rush off almost immediately—'

'If I go.'

Tricia's pretty little jaw dropped. 'What? What do you mean, *if* you go? Of *course* you're going! Linsey!'

She shrugged. 'Am I?'

Tricia sank back into her corner of the sofa, her eyes searching Linsey's face. 'Aren't you?'

'I don't know. He was hostile.'

'Hostile? Isn't that a bit strong?'

Linsey shook her head. 'No, I don't think so. I got the distinct feeling he thought I was a bubble-brain.'

Tricia laughed. 'What? You? A bubble-brain? Give it a rest!'

'I mean it.'

Tricia's smile faded. 'Lins, that's crazy. You're the most focused, intelligent, self-disciplined person I know—'

'Oh, Tricia!' Linsey laughed and hugged her friend. 'You are so loyal! I'm lazy, bird-brained and totally self-indulgent.'

Tricia shook her head emphatically. 'Only in the flat. You used to be like that, but you've spent years getting away from it. What you don't realise is you *have* got away—you're different now—and you most certainly aren't a bubble-brain.'

Linsey shrugged slightly. 'Tell it to Matthew Jarvis. He thinks I'm too daffy to do the job.'

'So why has he offered it to you?'

'Well, funny you should mention that. I really don't know.'

'But you will take it?'

Linsey hesitated. 'I have to earn a living,' she said

finally, 'and it is a lovely part of the world.'

Tricia studied her fingers for a moment. 'I'll miss you,' she murmured. 'You'll be a long way away.'

Linsey looked round the flat. 'Will you stay here?'

Tricia shrugged. 'Yes, probably. I'll see if I can get another flatmate—perhaps someone tidy?'

Linsey punched her arm gently and laughed. 'I'm not that bad any more.'

'No—but I've spent two years training you!'

'So you have.'

They shared a smile, and then Linsey bounced off the sofa and reached for the phone.

'What are you doing?'

'Accepting the job—quickly, before I talk myself out of it. Then you can help me pack.'

The traffic was awful. The last Saturday in July was the very worst time of year to make her way down through the New Forest, and by lunchtime Linsey was bitterly regretting her timing.

The motorway was chock-a-block, and when she finally left it the tailback to Lyndhurst was about five miles long and growing steadily.

She consulted her map, did a U-turn in the road and cut through the tiny villages, making a big circuit but saving herself probably at least one hot, frustrating hour of sitting in a traffic queue.

It was better then until after Brockenhurst, but the last bit into Lymington started to get very busy and she did another wiggle through the villages, cutting down through Sway and Pennington and picking up the coast road for Milhaven without having to wrestle with Lymington on market day—and that had to be good news.

Suzanne had warned her about market day when she'd made the final arrangements to come down, and as she saw the traffic heading back into Lymington from the west, she was heartily relieved that she wasn't on call and trying to fight with the traffic on her way to an emergency.

She pulled into the car park behind the surgery and found a space with her name on it, neatly painted onto a little white board on a short post hammered into the ground. Obediently, she parked in her slot and glanced across at the only other car there.

Matthew's? Suzanne had said someone would be there to let her in, give her the keys and show her how the alarm worked. She hadn't said who, though.

Only one way to find out, thought Linsey, but her legs seemed strangely reluctant all of a sudden. What if he was still hostile? Was it all going to have been the most dreadful mistake?

She shook her head in irritation, flung open the door and climbed out of the car. She was hot and sticky, her hair was tangled to death from driving with the windows open and she hoped that there were gallons of hot water because she was going to have the longest shower in the world—just as soon as she'd found the flat and got all her stuff inside.

Matthew watched from the attic as Linsey climbed out of the car, stretching her long, slender legs and shaking her hair out of her eyes. She looked hot and cross, he thought, and incredibly beautiful.

Damn. If those jeans fitted her any tighter they'd cut off her circulation. She opened the boot of her car and bent over, treating him to an inviting curve of taut bottom.

He groaned and dropped his forehead against the glass. What had he done? She was going to drive him crazy. The libido he'd managed so effectively to stifle with Jan's help roared healthily to life, kicking and screaming for recognition.

He shifted uncomfortably. His jeans were nearly as tight as hers now, damn it. She straightened, her full, soft breasts pushing against the limp T-shirt and making the ache worse.

'Oh, get a grip, Jarvis,' he growled. Turning away from the window, he ran down the stairs to the kitchen and opened the back door. 'You're here,' he said inanely, and could have kicked himself.

She looked up over her shoulder. 'So it appears,' she said drily. 'Did I misunderstand your letter?'

He felt a grin tug at the corner of his mouth and stepped down onto the gravel. 'Of course not. How was your journey?'

She gave him a withering look. 'How do you think? It's the busiest Saturday of the summer on the roads, and guess where everybody wants to be.'

The grin widened. 'I should have warned you. I'm sorry.'

'I'm sorry too. I hate traffic jams. Is there a shower?'

Matthew had a sudden, crystal-clear vision of Linsey naked under a stream of water, and his jeans tightened further. 'Yes,' he said curtly. 'There's a shower, and the hot water's on.'

She raised an eyebrow at his tone, but said nothing. Instead she turned her back to him, picked up the heaviest of the cases and dropped it almost on his toes.

'Here—you can prove you're a gentleman. I'll take the rest.'

She picked up two smaller cases and stood waiting

while he gathered his wits, picked up the case and headed for the door.

'Follow me,' he said unnecessarily, and all but ran up the stairs to the attic. He took the case straight into the bedroom, put it on the wide, solid bed and turned— straight into Linsey's soft, incredibly inviting chest. His hands came up to steady her, grabbing her shoulders and hauling her even tighter against him, and as he did so her mouth parted on a little gasp of surprise and he fell headlong into a boiling maelstrom of lust and forbidden fantasy.

Good grief, his eyes! Talk about hot and bothered. It was a wonder she hadn't melted clean away! Linsey dropped the cases and Matthew dropped her, stepping sharply backwards with a muttered oath and crashing into the wardrobe.

'Damn.' He wiggled his foot experimentally. 'What have you got in that case?'

'Books. I'm sorry. Are you all right?'

He swore softly again and rubbed the back of his head. 'I'll live.'

She felt a pang of guilt. 'Look, I can manage the rest. Why don't you give me the keys, show me the alarm and then you can go back to your wife and family?'

He stared at her. 'I don't have a wife and family.'

'Oh.' She blinked. 'I thought you were engaged.'

'I was—about a hundred years ago. Come and see the rest of the flat,' he muttered, and shot out through the door.

Linsey was rooted to the spot. Land's sakes! Well, she'd wondered about his wife. Now she knew.

A tiny, very feminine smile played around her lips as she followed him out of the bedroom and back onto the large, airy landing that formed her entrance.

It was decorated simply but tastefully, and as she looked in turn at the sitting room, with its squashy chairs and pretty chintz, the squeaky-clean kitchen with modern units and appliances and even a washer-dryer for clothes, and the bathroom, also squeaky-clean with a white suite, gleaming chrome taps and fresh, pretty floral curtains, she knew that she was going to be very much at home here. She was pleased to see the shower over the bath. Just as soon as he went, she would take advantage of it.

She went back into the sitting room, crossed to the window, and there, if she craned her neck, was the sea view that Rhys had promised. She turned to Matthew with a smile.

'It's lovely. How much will it cost me a month?'

He looked startled. 'Nothing. It's part of the deal.'

'Oh, but that's silly!'

He shrugged. 'We have our reasons. It helps us to have someone on the premises for security purposes, to act as a deterrent. We use it sometimes for locums, as well. Anyway, it stands empty, and we can't let it because it has access to the practice.'

She looked around the sitting room again. 'It's beautifully furnished just for the odd trainee or locum.'

His mouth quirked. 'I used to live here. I've got a cottage now three miles away on the outskirts of Sway, so I don't need it any more. Anyway, I have to confess the suite isn't that comfortable!' His mouth twitched again, and Linsey let herself return the almost-smile.

Heavens, he was practically unbending! Wonders would never cease.

'So, when do I start?' she asked him.

'The first of August is on Tuesday. I should spend

tomorrow and Monday getting to know the place—the roads, the practice. Poke around and look for things, and familiarise yourself with everything. Then on Tuesday I suggest you spend the day with me, shadowing me so you know what my day consists of. In fact the whole of this first week probably wouldn't be too long to do that, but I anticipate we can have you working almost independently in surgery hours after a couple of days.'

She looked at him in surprise. 'Why so long? In hospital you go in on the first day and take over from your predecessor. There's no induction time.'

He smiled wryly. 'Because I need to know you're able to do the job, and the best way for me to find that out is to let you work beside me at first.'

She arched a brow at him. 'Don't you trust me, Dr Jarvis?' she said pertly.

His reply was blunt. 'No, Dr Wheeler, I don't. Not until I've seen you working.'

That took the wind out of her sails. So, even more, did his next words.

'Why don't you go ahead and have that shower you were promising yourself? And I'll bring in the rest of your things out of the car and make you a cup of tea.'

Without waiting for a reply he turned and ran lightly down the stairs, and left her on the landing, mouth hanging open slightly. Shower? With him running in and out?

She shrugged. She was too hot to care. If he thought she should have a shower now, who was she to argue? She opened the case with her wash things in it, scooped up all the bathroomy bits and pieces and went out of the bedroom, just as he came back in.

This collision was just as spectacular. Her toiletries leapt out of her arms, tampons spraying across the landing as the box fell, and with a chuckle she sagged back against the wall and grinned at him.

'If I didn't know better I'd think you kept running into me on purpose,' she teased.

He looked up from the floor where he was busily cramming tampons back into the box, and she was fascinated to see the warm tide of colour creep over his skin.

My God, he's delectable, she thought. She bent down and took them out of his hands. 'Did you come back for anything in particular?' she asked softly.

'Car keys,' he mumbled. He straightened and stepped back, and the toothpaste tube ruptured and squirted across the landing, splattering the white wall with minty green.

He swore, comprehensively and not really very quietly, and glared at the dollops of toothpaste as they began to run slowly down the wall.

It was too much for Linsey. Folding up on the floor in a heap, she laughed until she cried, her sides aching and begging for mercy, her eyes streaming.

Around her Matthew stomped about, gathering up the remains of her wash things and dumping them in the basin in the bathroom, then going into the kitchen for a cloth to wipe the wall, all the while muttering under his breath.

When she could breathe again she looked up at him. 'Did you say something?' she wheezed, and giggled again as he glared at her. It was too much. The laughter bubbled up and over again, and she folded herself over her knees and sobbed with hilarity.

'I'm glad you're so damned amused,' he growled, almost stepping on her fingers as he wiped the wall for the third time.

She snatched them away to safety. 'At least the wall

won't get dental decay,' she said brightly, and his scowl set her off again.

At last she straightened and sat back on her heels. 'Oh, come on. Can't you see the funny side?' she pleaded.

He tried hard, but finally, to her enormous relief, his face cracked and he smiled, albeit rather ruefully. 'Keys?' he said softly.

She knelt up and delved in her jeans pocket. 'Here. There isn't much. I'll have that shower now, if you think you can manage not to knock me over this time.'

His eyes seemed to darken, or perhaps it was just a trick of the light. Anyway, with a mumbled comment about keeping out of her way he turned and was gone, leaving her kneeling in the middle of the landing surrounded by the lingering aroma of toothpaste and wondering if she'd imagined that look in his eyes.

'This is your consulting room. It's next to mine on purpose so that if you want to confer with me you can do so easily. I imagine we'll work closely together for some time.'

So he can't delegate. We'll see about that, she thought. 'Is it really necessary?' she asked.

He looked at her candidly. 'I don't know. We'll find out, won't we? Come and see the little theatre where we do our minor surgery.'

She followed him. 'Who does it?'

'Me or Rhys. No one else is qualified. You'll meet Tim this week, and Rosie, but she's leaving in a couple of months and she's only part-time.'

'Is that why you offered me the job? Because a woman's leaving and you had to have the statutory woman doctor?'

She had stopped in her tracks and he turned and looked

back at her, irritation etched on his face. 'We didn't *have* to have a woman. We felt it would be a good idea. Many women prefer to see another woman for gynae problems. Obstetrics, for some reason, is different. They don't mind when it's babies, but when it's periods and the menopause and discharges they get coy.'

'Naturally. Men, on the other hand, are always coy unless they're trying to jump your bones. Then they all but hand you a tape-measure.'

He couldn't stop the stunned cough of laughter that erupted from his lips. Oh, good, she thought, he does have a sense of humour, after all.

'Lady, you are wicked,' he informed her, but his eyes twinkled and she found herself unexpectedly drawn to him again.

Maybe her fantasy hero did exist, after all. Not only that, he was single. She had the distinct feeling it was going to be an interesting year. . .

CHAPTER THREE

MATTHEW was going crazy.

Every time he turned around Linsey was there, asking him questions, watching what he did, poking about in the files, running through the computer data, questioning everything—and it was still only Monday! God knows what it would be like once they started working together properly. He had never before come across anyone with a mind as enquiring and convoluted as hers, and he found it exhausting.

Lack of sleep didn't help either. Every time he closed his eyes she was there, singing in the shower, her voice slightly off-key, her body glistening as she slicked soap over that fabulous peach-bloom skin. Whose idea had it been to put frosted glass in the top of the bathroom door anyway? That one diffuse glimpse of her upraised arms had been enough to wreck his sleep pattern in perpetuity.

Hell.

He signed the last repeat prescription and then turned to the pile of letters awaiting signature. Just as he checked the first there was a tap on the door.

'Come in,' he growled.

Linsey popped her head round. 'Just thought I'd check the arrangements for tomorrow,' she told him.

'Eight-fifteen, in here,' he reiterated. 'I'll introduce you to my patients, and then conduct the consultations as normal.'

'And what do I do?'

'Nothing,' he said firmly. 'Absolutely nothing

45

whatsoever except watch and listen and answer questions if I ask them.'

'What if I disagree?'

He sighed inwardly. 'You won't.'

Her brows arched expressively, and he glared at her.

'It isn't me we're supposed to be checking up on,' he reminded her stiffly.

'But if I do disagree? If, for instance, I would have treated something differently? Surely we should discuss it?'

'Later. When the patient leaves.'

She nodded, and he had visions of five-minute consultations followed by ten-minute wrangles over the efficacy of his chosen course of treatment. He sighed again, this time audibly, and she caught her teeth in her lip. Self-doubt, or trying to hide a smile? He didn't care to consider it too closely.

'Doesn't anybody ever question anything you do?' she asked.

'Oh, yes. The patients do it all the time. I can reason with them, though,' he finished drily. He looked pointedly at his watch. 'Was there anything else?'

She pulled a face. 'Well, excuse me,' she said cheekily, and with a sniff she turned and went out, banging the door oh, so softly behind her.

He smiled. He didn't mean to, but the thing sort of snuck up on him. Damn, but she was going to be a feisty little handful.

That was a bad choice of words. His hands longed for the soft, heavy feel of her breasts. He could still feel their imprint on his chest after their first collision on Saturday.

He swore softly, dragged his mind back to the letters and forced himself to concentrate, just long enough to finish them. Then he took himself home for the night and prayed for oblivion. God knows, he thought, I'll need a decent night's sleep to deal with that aggravating witch tomorrow.

Linsey stood in bra, pants and tights and glared at the contents of her wardrobe. For heaven's sake, it didn't matter what she wore! She was dressing for work, not for Matthew!

Irritated beyond belief by her own stupidity, she snatched out the first thing she came across, only to stop as she was tugging it over her head. A wool mix? In a heatwave? Good grief. She put the dress back, removed instead a cotton skirt and matching sleeveless vest-top. It was going to be a scorcher today. In fact, her tights were a mistake. She wriggled out of them, pulled on the skirt and top and slid her feet into cool, strappy sandals. There.

Now, if she could just persuade her hair to stay up in a professional-looking bun instead of slithering down her back as usual, she would be fine.

She headed for the stairs. Would Matthew be in a grouch this morning, or would she see another side of him? She laid odds on the grouch, and wasn't disappointed.

He greeted her with a reserved smile and a reminder that she was there to observe, and so she watched him as he checked his post, ripped open an envelope and scanned the contents, scribbled a note for Suzanne and took another swig of coffee.

'Riveting stuff,' she said drily after about ten minutes.

He glanced up, shook his head and apologised. 'Sorry. I'm a bit pushed this morning—I had a couple of calls to make on the way here. I normally get this out of the way by eight. Grab a coffee; I'll be with you in a minute.'

She went out to the kitchen and encountered a stranger. She studied him for a second—slight, dark, late twenties—and smiled. 'You must be Tim Wilson.'

He nodded. 'And you're Linsey. Wonderful. I can have a day off at last.'

She chuckled. 'I shouldn't bank on it. So far I'm not even allowed to sharpen a pencil.'

Tim grinned. 'He'll unbend. He likes his trainees to know their place.'

'I like my trainees to know the job,' Matthew corrected him mildly from behind Linsey. 'That way I know I can rely on them. How did you get on with Mrs James?'

'Oh, OK. She's stable. I wondered if we might have to transfer her to Lymington, but I think she'll be all right in Milhaven, at least for now. I'll go and see her again later.'

Matthew nodded. 'Fine. Right, Linsey, when you're ready. . .'

She was every bit as difficult as he had anticipated. She sat there, cool and delectable and good enough to eat, her bare, satiny legs tormenting him every time she moved, and she said nothing.

Her face, however, was far from silent. Not a poker player, he thought; and after each patient came the barrage of questions.

'Why did you tell her to come back in a week if it's no better? You know it'll be better.'

'Because she's a worrier and she likes support.'

'Why did you give him a prescription? Why not just tell him he had a virus and didn't need anything?'

'Because he would just come back again and again until he had a prescription. He always does.'

This went on all morning, until at eleven-fifteen the surgery finally ground to a halt. They went into the kitchen for coffee and she started again.

'None of your reasons are medical. None of these treatments I've queried have been suggested on medical grounds!'

'No,' he replied mildly. 'But I'm treating the patient and not the condition. That's general practice—that's what your precious continuity of care gives you, Linsey: an opportunity to know your patient so well you can out-psych him or her.'

'But I can't do that yet! I would have told Mrs Bates to go home and that she'd be fine, and I would have sent Mr Dean off without a prescription for antibiotics, with an explanation of his condition. Does that make me a better doctor, or a worse one?'

'Neither. Just different. Anyway, his prescription wasn't for antibiotics,' Matthew told her with what felt to him suspiciously like childish glee. 'It was for a para-cetamol-based painkiller. They'll reduce his symptoms, he'll get better anyway, and he won't come back and waste our time.'

She rolled her eyes. 'Why not just tell him to take paracetamol and have done with it?'

Matthew smiled. 'Because he'd say it wouldn't work. He's just a big baby, Linsey. He likes to be molly-coddled. He's happy, and that means I'm happy. What have I done that's so wrong?'

'You're sneaky,' she said huffily, and he wanted to hug her.

Instead he drained his coffee and stood up. 'Come on; visits now.'

'More of the same?' she said wryly.

He grinned. 'Probably.'

It wasn't, though. One of the patients was elderly and had been suffering 'a spot of indigestion'. By the time they arrived he was in severe pain, breathless, cyanosed and obviously having a major heart attack. While Matthew arranged his admission to Lymington Hospital with its twenty-four-hour medical presence, rather than Milhaven which only had GP call-out cover, Linsey gave him an intravenous injection of diamorphine to kill the pain, and gradually his face relaxed. However, his colour was still bad and while they waited Matthew rigged up the portable oxygen cylinder he carried in his car and Linsey sat and talked to him, calming him with her quiet words.

Damn it, she was good with him, Matthew acknowledged. Perhaps her references were believable, after all. He watched, one eye on the window for the ambulance, and moments later it arrived and whisked the old boy off to Lymington.

Matthew scribbled in the notes, then pocketed his pen. 'I'll just tell his neighbour—she's got a key, so she can come in and feed the cat and keep an eye on the place. I expect she'll visit him. She's been a treasure since his wife died six months ago.'

There was no reply, and Matthew looked up to find that Linsey was standing holding a faded picture of a young couple on their wedding day. 'Is this them?' she asked, her voice a little scratchy.

Matthew looked at her carefully, then glanced at the photograph. 'Yes, it is.'

She put the picture down with great care and stared around her at the spacious but lonely bedroom. Evidence of Mr Roland's late wife was all around—pictures, a tapestry she had done, even a favourite cardigan folded on a chair, gathering dust.

'I've never seen their homes,' she said, and she sounded a little awed and somewhat sad. 'They came from out of nowhere, and we sent them back without any idea of whether they could cope and what their conditions were like.'

Matthew snorted. 'Tell me about it. We had one chap who had a prostate operation as a day case and was sent home with bladder irrigation for the first forty-eight hours! And who was supposed to do it? Me and the district nurse.'

'So what did you do?'

He sighed. 'I admitted him to the cottage hospital and he was properly looked after. I expect they knew we'd do that. Anyway, I wrote with some—ah, suggestions, and they've since changed their procedures.'

Linsey met his eyes and returned his smile. 'I'll bet,' she said softly. 'I'll just bet.'

He dragged his eyes away from hers and cleared his throat. 'Right, two more calls and then we can pop in at the hospital on our way back for lunch.'

They paused for a quick chat with the neighbour, did a post-op follow-up and another visit to a sick child with tonsillitis, and then popped into the cottage hospital.

A between-the-wars structure, it was on two floors, with two small wards and a tiny casualty unit for very minor problems, which doubled as an out-patient clinic for minor-surgery techniques by those GPs who didn't have their own facilities, Matthew explained. There were thirty beds altogether in the two wards, both mixed, although the patients were 'zoned' to give them a little more privacy.

The lady they were to check on was in the ground-floor ward at the far end, and she was lying chatting happily with the lady in the next bed.

'Hello, Mrs Simms,' Matthew said cheerfully.

'Oh, Doctor! Hello. Oh, my goodness, I wasn't expecting you—let me put my teeth in.'

She fumbled in the pot by the bed, and then gave them a toothy grin and shuffled up the bed a little. 'There. That's better. How are you?'

Matthew grinned and winked at the neighbour. 'I thought that was my line.'

She laughed. 'Oh, well—it is! And I'm much better, but I shouldn't tell you that or you'll send me home,' she confided with a wheezy giggle. Her eyes flicked to Linsey. 'Who's your girlfriend, Dr Jarvis?'

Matthew felt the colour threaten and could have strangled the old dear for her choice of words. 'I should be so lucky,' he said lightly. 'This is Dr Wheeler, who's been working in hospitals until now and is spending a year with us in general practice.'

She patted his arm. 'A whole year, eh? I expect you'll manage to charm her in that time, dear, don't you?'

She gave another wheezy cackle and Matthew found his smile was slipping a little. Linsey, bless her, moved up beside him and shook Mrs Simms's hand, relieving him of the necessity for a reply. Her words, though, did nothing to soothe him.

'It's nice to meet you, Mrs Simms,' she said with a smile. 'I expect I'll be seeing quite a bit of you one way and another, and I'll keep you in touch with his progress—although I must say he's been a bit lacking on the charm front recently. Perhaps we'll have to give him some lessons.'

He thought the old duck was going to be pushing up daisies, she laughed so much. He glared at Linsey, who simply smiled innocently and stepped back out of his way, eyes sparkling with mischief.

He arched a brow at her disapprovingly, ignored her tiny giggle of defiance and whipped his stethoscope out of his pocket. 'Right, Mrs Simms, let's have a listen to this old chest of yours and see if it's a bit clearer.' He turned to Linsey. 'She had a touch of right-sided failure and a bit of oedema, so we're keeping an eye on the chest, and her legs are supposed to be up to aid her venous return and get the oedema down. Isn't that right?'

'If you say so, Doctor. Do you want my nightie up?'

He shook his head. 'No, I can hear through the material if you'll stop cracking jokes with my colleague,' he growled gently.

She pulled a mock-guilty face, breathed in and out obediently and showed him her legs. He passed the stethoscope to Linsey. 'There's a little congestion still in the lower left lobe of her lungs. Otherwise she seems clear. Have a listen.'

She did so, frowning as she handed him back the instrument. He shook his head slightly in warning and tucked Mrs Simms back up in the bed. 'Right, my dear, I think you can go home if you promise to wear your support tights and take your water tablets. Do you think you can do that?'

'Oh, it's been so warm to wear tights, and I forget the pills—'

'I can always send you to Southampton,' he said mildly, folding up the stethoscope and returning it to his pocket.

'No—no, I'll do it. I really will, I promise!'

He smiled at her and patted her hand. 'All right. You can go home just as soon as someone can get you some food in and give you a lift, all right? How about your son?'

'I'll ask him. He's in this afternoon—could I go then?'

'Yes, if he can sort it out. I'll sign your forms and they can get your pills ready, OK? And I'll come and see you at home in a few days.'

He ushered Linsey out and made sure they were well out of earshot before he let her speak. 'Well?' he said.

'Her heart's a bit rough, isn't it?'

He smiled. 'Just a bit. I don't think she has any idea how irregular the beat is or how weak. I don't want her to know, either. She's a sweet old thing and she's near the end—I don't want her to have to worry every minute.'

He did the necessary paperwork in the sister's office on the way out, and then whipped the professional journal that Linsey had picked up off the desk from her hand and ushered her out of the door.

'Lunchtime,' he said succinctly. They reached the car and he unlocked it, and the blast of heat from the inside nearly choked him. Their eyes met over the roof. 'How about picking up a sandwich and eating it in the park over the road? Maybe we can find a patch of shade.'

She looked doubtful. 'Have we got time?'

'Just about.'

He shut the car door again, but as he did so a woman ran from the hospital entrance. 'Dr Jarvis? Wait!'

He turned towards her. 'Yes?'

'Call from the surgery—would you please go straight back there—there's an emergency come in and no one's there. Someone's collapsed with the heat and the receptionist said another patient was resuscitating her.'

He unlocked the car, jumped in, regardless of the temperature and gunned the engine, pulling away in a squeal of tyres. He just hoped Linsey was in, because there wasn't time to worry about her. He shot her a quick glance. 'OK? Sorry about that.'

She shrugged. 'That's medicine for you. One minute you're planning lunch in the park, the next you're flying along at fifty in a thirty-mile-an-hour limit to save someone's life. It's about time it hotted up—it's been a bit tame really so far.'

He laughed. 'Tame? That's general practice for you, Linsey. Old dears and tonsils.'

He swung into the surgery car park, cut the engine and ran, leaving the door hanging open. He didn't wait for Linsey. There wasn't time.

They needn't have hurried. The woman, in her late fifties and heavily obese, had succumbed to the heat and nothing and no one could bring her back. They had no idea who she was, except that she wasn't local. She had been dropped off at the gate by someone, Linsey gathered—possibly a taxi. She was wearing a wedding ring round her neck, but whether because she was divorced or because her fingers had become so swollen that she could no longer get it on they had no idea.

'No ID at all,' Matthew said in disgust. 'Oh, well, she'd better go to Lymington Hospital mortuary.'

'Don't you have a mortuary here?' Linsey asked.

'Yes, but it's not chilled, and in this heat—' He shrugged. 'We may have to keep her body some time before we can identify her, and she'll need a post-mortem, even though the cause of death is fairly obvious. That has to be done at Lymington. And in the meantime, we have to wait for someone to notice that she's missing.'

'Poor old thing,' Linsey said. 'Fancy dying like that, all alone. Do you suppose she's here on holiday?'

'Could be. We won't know, will we? I'll notify the police.'

He disappeared, leaving Linsey with the dead woman, and she searched the body yet again for any clues. There was only one—the label on the blouse was not mass-produced, nor was the garment, and it declared that the blouse was made in Sussex by Christine Cleary.

A clue? Possibly. She knew the name, and the firm. She wrote it down and gave the piece of paper to Suzanne. 'Could you give this to the police? They're a small local firm specialising in outsize clothes. It might be worth contacting them. My aunt uses them, and they're very good at remembering her name. Perhaps they'll know this lady, unless she picked up the blouse at a jumble sale or second-hand shop. They might be worth speaking to.'

Suzanne took the piece of paper and promised to hand the information on. By this time Matthew had finished with the police on the phone and the ambulance had arrived to move the body.

He shot a glance at his watch. 'Looks like lunch will be a quick cup of coffee and yet another packet of biscuits,' he said with a sigh.

Linsey needed more than that. Slender she might be, but there was a lot of her, nonetheless. 'Speak for yourself—I'm having something out of my fridge.'

He looked at her as if she held the elixir of life in her hands. 'Is there enough for two?' he said hopefully.

She chuckled. 'Maybe. I could knock up a cheese salad,' she offered.

His eyes lit up. 'Really? I'm ravenous. I didn't have time for breakfast,' he confessed.

She shook her head disapprovingly and ran upstairs to her flat, Matthew on her heels. They raided the fridge and he grated cheese while she washed and cut up the salad, then they bolted the food down and went back to the kitchen to grab a mug of filter coffee before the antenatal clinic started at two. They hadn't had time to exchange more than a word or two, but nevertheless, sharing the meal had been cosy in a way, and she hoped it might have softened him up, because there was something she wanted, and he needed to be receptive.

'Can I ask a favour?' she said, wondering how he would react.

'You give me lunch and already you want a favour?'

She blushed a little, and he laughed.

'I knew it. What?'

'Can I do your antenatal clinic?'

'No.'

Fine. That was how he'd react, of course. Why had she expected anything different?

He leant over and covered her hand with his, and a shiver went up her arm as he squeezed gently and released her. 'Watch what I do, how I work with the midwife—by all means ask questions and, if the mums don't mind, examine them, but I want to make sure you do things our way.' He looked at her, saw the set of her mouth and she could see the conciliatory words forming in his mind.

'It's not that I don't trust you.' She mimicked his voice.

He grinned sheepishly. 'It isn't. You said yourself continuity was important. Just give yourself a few days to settle in and you'll find you've got more than enough to keep you quiet. Rosie's going on holiday in a fortnight, and Tim is owed time off in a serious way. Don't worry, Linsey. Just enjoy the rest while it lasts.'

So she did. Well, in a manner of speaking. While he dealt with one patient, she read through the notes of the next, then observed to see if he followed up the way she would have done.

He did. She was relieved. After the morning's episode with the carefully nurtured psyches of his neurotic patients, she had wondered if she was cut out for general practice.

Halfway through, the phone rang.

'Would you get that, please, Dr Wheeler?' Matthew asked, continuing to palpate the distended abdomen of his patient.

She picked up the phone. 'Yes?'

'Could you ask Dr Jarvis to phone Dr Williams at home as soon as possible, Dr Wheeler?' April, the receptionist, asked her.

'Of course. Any idea what about?'

'He didn't say, but it sounded urgent.'

'I'll hand it on,' she promised.

As she cradled the receiver Matthew raised one eyebrow at her.

'Phone Dr Williams at home.'

He nodded, finished the consultation and picked up the phone.

'Rhys? Matthew. What can I do for you?'

He leant back in the chair, listening for a moment. 'Sure. What sort of problem?'

There was a short silence. 'Judy? What about her?'

Another pause, then Matthew straightened slowly. 'Gone? Where to?'

Linsey caught the anxiety in his voice, and turned to him. 'Problems?' she mouthed.

He nodded. 'Of course. I'll be there in ten minutes.'

He put the phone down, grabbed his jacket and rummaged for the car keys. 'You get your wish. Could you finish my antenatal clinic, please? And you might find you get twice as lucky and end up doing Rhys's surgery this evening, if not for the rest of the week. His wife's just left him.'

As a parting shot, Linsey thought, it was superb. The rest of the afternoon passed in a blur of activity, and as she tried desperately to do things as Matthew would have done without compromising her own judgement she found her mind straying to the big, genial man who had shown her such kindness on the day of her interview.

What kind of personal hell was he going through now? Why had his wife left him? He seemed such a genuinely decent man. Was it all a sham? Perhaps he beat her. Maybe he drank—plenty of doctors did, given the stress of the job.

The last antenatal patient came and went, and Linsey went out to Reception with the bundle of notes and spoke to Suzanne. 'Any news from Dr Williams or Dr Jarvis?'

'Yes—can you please do Rhys's evening surgery? He's on call tonight but Matthew says Tim'll do that. Will you be able to manage?'

'Of course. Where are the notes? Perhaps I should look through them first and see if there's anything I should be aware of.'

She was handed a stack of patient envelopes and went into her consulting room. Her name was on the door, she noticed, and it all looked very professional. She was qualified, her last stint had been in A and E and she'd had more than enough responsibility there.

So why were her hands clammy and her knees knocking and why was her heart beating nineteen to the dozen? All day she'd been frustrated by the lack of responsibility. So why the sudden stage fright?

Oh, well, perhaps the adrenalin would help her to

concentrate and do things right. At least she was com-
puter-literate! So many of her hospital colleagues
hadn't been.

She flicked on the monitor, tapped buttons and
brought the notes of the first patient up on the screen.
An elderly lady with apparently very good health, she
had no immediate history that Linsey thought could be
troubling her. So, no clues. Oh, well.

She checked the second patient, and the third, with
the same result, and finally decided that the way to
handle it was to scan the notes just before the patient
came in. She could hear Matthew's voice, and was
reassured to know he was just the other side of the wall
and could be summoned in the event of any difficulty.

That was the difference, of course. In hospital there
was always another person on the next rung of the ladder
who could be referred to at a moment's notice. A GP
had to make all the decisions and carry the can totally
alone. It was a lonely life, she realised, and could be
stressful not only because of the pressure but the tedium
and very autonomy of it.

The rewards, on the other hand, were more readily
visible than in hospital. Children cared for from an early
stage of pregnancy would stay in the practice and
become adults, and would in turn bring their children
in. Family doctoring at its best.

And she was just about to taste it for the first time. . .

CHAPTER FOUR

MATTHEW was waiting for her in the kitchen when she finished her surgery just after six-thirty. He didn't say a word, just pushed a mug of coffee across the table towards her and watched in silence as she sipped it gratefully, wriggled her feet out of her shoes and sighed.

'Manage OK?' he asked at last.

She nodded.

'Any problems?'

She shook her head. 'No, I don't think so.'

He looked almost disappointed, she thought, and nearly smiled. Then she remembered why she had been doing the surgery in the first place, and the urge to smile vanished.

'How's Rhys?' she asked softly.

Matthew's face darkened. 'Shattered. Can we go up to your flat?'

'Sure.' She drained her coffee, picked up her shoes and led the way upstairs. The sun was dipping in the sky, glinting on the distant sea, and she stood in the window and breathed in the cooler evening air. Finally she turned to him as he sprawled in the big armchair that she guessed had always been his favourite.

'So, tell me about Rhys.'

He shook his head. 'I can't—not all of it. He'll have to tell you himself. I'll tell you what I can, but it's not much. Judy's gone—walked out this morning, leaving a note. The kids were with a child-minder.'

How dreadful, to come home and find that, she

61

thought. She perched on the edge of the sofa near him. 'No warning?' she asked.

Matthew shrugged. 'Things hadn't been wonderful for a while. I don't think he made any secret of that, but no, there was no warning that she was going, certainly not like this, without saying anything or leaving an address.'

Linsey's eyes widened. 'But what about the children? Will she come back? Is it just a temporary escape from a difficult situation?'

Matthew sighed and ran his hands through his hair, rumpling it yet again. 'No, she won't come back. She made that clear, and he made it equally clear that he wouldn't have her. That does, of course, have implications for his job until he can set up some child-care arrangements.'

He smiled wearily at her. 'It seems, young lady, that you arrived in the nick of time. If you really coped all right with that surgery, then if you're happy to take it I'd like to hand some of Rhys's workload over to you now. Tim and Rosie and I will take the follow-up cases if you could see the one-offs and temporary residents, and we won't expect you to cover his out-of-hours work, but if you could simply do his routine surgeries and daytime visits it would help enormously.'

'Of course I will,' she agreed instantly. 'I imagine I'll start first thing in the morning. I could do with a street map if I'm to do his visits.'

'Suzanne will give you one. The other problem is your tutorials, but we'll just have to fit them in—in the evening, if necessary—after work. It won't be for long, but I'm unhappy about flinging you in at the deep end without support in your first practice appointment.'

She smiled reassuringly. 'Matthew, don't worry; I can cope.'

'Timing is difficult—keeping the appointments running smoothly without getting behind. It's so easy to get twenty minutes behind—one phone call, a slightly longer consultation, and it screws up the whole day.'

'I'm used to timing. I've done clinic work.'

'Any patients you're worried about, just come and see me.'

'I will.'

'Anything you're worried about—'

'Matthew?'

'Yes?'

'Don't stress.'

His mouth closed with a snap. Shutting his eyes, he tipped his head back and sighed. 'Sorry. It's just that being the senior partner has its responsibilities, and I take my responsibilities seriously.'

'So do I, so you can relax. Are you going to eat tonight? I could fling something together for us both, if you like.'

'Me?' He sat up and shrugged. 'I was going to eat, but rather than you feeding us again, why don't I take you out for a quick bite at the pub up the road? We can eat in the garden and if we're really lucky the New Forest ponies won't come and steal it all.'

A date? Well, there's a thing, she thought. She answered his smile with one of her own. 'Sounds good. Can you give me ten minutes to shower and change?'

'Sure.' He leapt to his feet and strode across the landing. 'I'll wait for you downstairs. I've got a few things to do.'

She watched his head disappear down the stairs, and grinned. Clearly the thought of her and her toiletries terrified the life out of him. Perhaps he thought she'd spray him with tampons and toothpaste again.

With a chuckle, she went into the bathroom, stripped into the laundry basket and turned the shower on full. She washed her hair as well. It had been too hot and sticky a day to leave it, and she could always brush it out and leave it to dry.

She dressed in light cotton leggings and a matching T-shirt, soft slip-on cotton shoes and a stroke of mascara. She didn't bother with lipstick as they were going to be eating, and she never wore eye-shadow anyway. Her hair was tangled, of course, and took ages to comb out, so she left it damp over her shoulders. It was still muggy, she decided, so she would hardly catch a chill, even if such a thing were possible.

She ran downstairs, only five minutes late, and tapped on his consulting-room door.

'Come in,' he grunted, and she opened the door and found him submerged in a sea of notes.

'Just sorting out tomorrow's surgery,' she was told. 'I'm almost done. Grab a pew.'

'I'll dry my hair. Come and get me when you're ready,' she said, and ran upstairs again. Lord, the stairs would get her fit, she thought with a smile. Up, down, up, down.

She was on the landing, bent over double, waving the hair-dryer at her hair, when she saw his feet behind her through her legs. She straightened up, throwing her hair over her head and turning. 'Ready?'

He cleared his throat. 'Um—yes. Got everything? Keys?'

She nodded, and he turned on his heel and went back down the stairs as if the hounds of hell were after him. Linsey chewed her lip and followed him at a more digni-

fied pace. Either he was having difficulty keeping his
hands off her, she decided, or he was scared of her. Since
she couldn't imagine Matthew being scared of anyone,
that left only one, rather intriguing possibility. . .

He was going to disgrace himself. She was glorious, her
hair gleaming gold in the evening sun, her face innocent
of make-up, her body sleek and slender yet softly curv-
ing. And that laugh!

It curled round his insides and turned him to mush.
Well, perhaps not mush. In fact, the opposite. He longed
for his tight, concealing jeans that were so good at
disguising his reaction.

They turned into the pub car park and saw a crowd
of people standing round, cameras clicking busily as
they stared at something in the middle of the road in
front of the pub.

Linsey was immediately curious, to Matthew's relief.
It took her attention away from him and might give him
time to control his libido.

'What *are* they photographing?' she asked in
amazement.

'I'll lay you odds it's a pony,' he said drily. They
crossed to the crowd and peered into the centre.

'Oh, Matthew, a foal! It can only be minutes old!'

Matthew snorted. 'Typical woman—having her baby
right in the middle of the road.' But he couldn't keep
the smile off his face, and when she turned, eyes shining,
his gut clenched and he had an almost overwhelming
urge to drag her into his arms and hug her.

And that was just for starters! He turned away from
the crowd, and with a last lingering look at the still-wet
foal Linsey followed him through the gate into the pub's
garden. There were several picnic tables scattered about

under birch trees, and because of all the interest in the foal's arrival they were able to find a table at the side of the garden, overlooking the open forest.

At least, Linsey was overlooking the forest. Matthew was overlooking Linsey, and his hormones were giving him hell. . .

It was a lovely meal. Matthew was a little preoccupied, Linsey thought, but put it down to worry over Rhys. Nevertheless, he was attentive. He told her about the practice, and how the work pattern had changed and shifted over the years, how a group of GPs had got together and installed a gastroenterology screening unit in the cottage hospital and how ulcers, bowel cancers and other related problems were now detected and sorted out much quicker.

He told her about the increase in the number of temporary residents they treated, and how the Forest was reaching saturation point with visitors, although the numbers in campsites were heavily restricted and well controlled, how the ancient paths and tracks were being destroyed because of the endless pony-trekking, and how the heathland in between the paths was steadily eroding due to the mass invasion that happened every year.

There were too many animals grazing too little grass, the recent droughts had caused even more problems, and she learned that the delightful ponies all belonged to someone and weren't truly wild at all.

'The Commoners, as the forest people are called, have the right to graze their animals on the common land. Each year in the autumn the stock are rounded up, the foals are counted and freezemarked with the owner's brand and young stock are sold on.'

'They must get killed on the road,' Linsey said, her

eyes still on the little foal who was struggling to stand with his mother's help.

'A lot of them do. The mothers cross the road, a car comes and the foals panic and try and rush across. A staggering number don't make it. I can't remember how many of the ponies are lost each year to road-traffic accidents, but it's a lot, and of course quite often, in high-speed night collisions, for instance, the occupants of the cars are hurt too.'

'But there are speed limits—I've seen yellow signs painted on the roads.'

Matthew shrugged. 'Only forty miles an hour—and that's too fast at night. Anyway, people break the limit all the time. No, the ponies are an attraction, of course, but they're also a hazard, both to themselves and to the visitors. People will feed them, and so they bite and kick and visitors get injured and blame the ponies, which is silly.'

Linsey looked at the fence around the garden. 'Do they get into people's gardens and damage the plants?'

Matthew grinned. 'Only if people leave the gates open. Nearly everyone has gates or a cattle-grid—sometimes both.'

'Do you?'

He laughed. 'Oh, yes, I've got a gate, and a stockproof hedge all round the garden—I need it. The ponies graze right up to the boundary all round.'

'Don't you have any neighbours?' Linsey asked in surprise.

He shook his head. 'No immediate neighbours, no. It's down a little wooded track and it's very much on its own. It was chosen for its isolation by the previous owner.'

'And why did you choose it?' Linsey asked, insatiably curious as ever.

His face twisted slightly. 'I didn't. He left it to me.'

Linsey felt her eyes widen. 'He left it to you? Why? Was he a relative?'

Matthew shook his head. 'No, not a relative. Not even a friend, really, until the end. He was a patient—a homosexual with AIDS-related complex. When he found out, he cut himself off from all his London friends, retreated to his little cottage and waited to die. He was here three years altogether, and he left me the cottage because he said I was the only person who understood how he felt, who didn't patronise or pass judgement or overdramatise. We used to play chess and shred up the current politics and tell awful jokes and generally pass the time.'

'Was he rich?'

Matthew shrugged. 'So-so, I suppose. He was a playwright. He was still working right up to the end. He had a brilliant mind—tortuous. And he was a very lonely man. The loneliest person I've ever met.'

'And you became his only friend.' Linsey swallowed. 'How sad.'

'I like to think I made a bit of difference.'

Linsey thought of the unknown man's situation, and how Matthew's company and acceptance must have eased his pain. 'I'm sure you did,' she murmured.

She took a big breath. 'So—tell me about it. Is it big? Small?'

'Quite small. One big sitting room, kitchen just large enough to eat in, two bedrooms and a bathroom.'

'Is it brick?'

'Good heavens, no. Wattle and daub over a timber frame, and thatch.'

'Oh, it sounds lovely! Can I see it?'

'Now?' he said, looking a bit taken aback.

'Yes—why not?'

He chuckled ruefully. 'Because I didn't make the bed this morning, I probably haven't washed up from last night and my cleaning lady comes on Wednesday.'

'So?'

'So it's Tuesday. That's bad news.'

She laughed. 'Tricia, my flatmate, calls me a pack-rat. She says I'm the dirtiest, untidiest, least domesticated person she's ever lived with, so please don't worry on my account!'

'Your flat looked fine,' he said in surprise.

'So, she's trained me! And anyway, I haven't been here long enough to get a real mess under way.'

He chuckled, and she let her smile blossom. It was good to see him relax. Maybe he was going to let her see the cottage, after all.

He tipped his head at her plate. 'Have you finished?'

She nodded.

'Right, I'll settle up and see you at the car. I expect you're going to talk to the Forest's latest arrival, are you?'

She laughed and agreed. Was she so easy to read?

'Be careful,' he warned her. 'The mother might kick if you get too close. She'll be very protective.'

So Linsey went and stood a few yards away and watched the little chap struggle to his feet, his mother nudging him with her nose to assist his unskilled efforts, and she went gooey inside when he started to suckle, his little tail wiggling furiously like a lamb's.

She heard footsteps behind her, and the mare turned her head curiously and watched as Matthew approached.

'It's a late foal,' he told her. 'It's missed the spring grass, so it'll find the winter hard unless they keep it in.

More and more people are doing that.'

'It's gorgeous.'

Matthew smiled. 'Softy,' he said gently.

'I am.' She turned away and smiled up at him, her eyes misty. She felt silly, but the little scrap had got to her. Obstetrics had always been her weakness, she thought with a little laugh. 'Come on, then. Show me your Hansel and Gretel cottage in the woods.'

It was a short drive away, less than a mile, and when they turned down the narrow, unmade track she could see what Matthew meant about isolation.

The cottage was totally invisible from the main road, and it was only as they approached that she caught her first glimpse of it.

White-painted, the thatch low down over the eaves, with little dormers like raised eyebrows interrupting the line of the roof, it was enchanting. Roses scrambled over the walls and up the thatch, and the beds around the walls were a blaze of colour.

She hopped out to open the gate and closed it again behind the car, mindful of the small group of ponies that they had passed, standing idly swishing their tails just yards away on the track. No doubt they would sell their souls to get their teeth into Matthew's garden!

He pulled up in front of the cottage and stood waiting for her as she crossed the lawn. 'Well?' he said expectantly.

She didn't disappoint him. 'It's gorgeous. Absolutely fairy-tale. I want to see inside.'

'God, what a demanding woman,' he said mildly, but he unlocked the door and ushered her in.

It was white-painted, the carpet a soft old gold, almost honey-coloured, and everything was either very pale, or dark, like the beams. An ancient oak chest stood against one wall, a grandfather clock against another. Grouped around the inglenook was a pair of sofas in pale cream, and between them was a lovely old Persian rug in soft, faded blues and golds.

'Everything is exactly as Joe left it,' Matthew told her. 'I didn't have any money to do anything, and it wasn't necessary.'

'Did he leave everything in the cottage to you as well?'

He nodded. 'Yes. I gave his personal effects to his parents, and I gather they burned them. I wish I'd kept them now, but I thought they'd want them.'

'They must have been hurt, perhaps by his unconventional lifestyle.'

'His sexuality, you mean. They never forgave him. His mother accused him of getting AIDS just to torture her.'

'How sad.' Linsey ran her fingers over the top of the oak chest, feeling the lovely mellow patina of age.

'Checking for dust?' Matthew teased.

She smiled wistfully. 'No. I just love old things.'

'I'm an old thing.'

She turned to him, her heart suddenly thudding in her chest. 'So you are,' she said lightly.

His eyes were burning up again, and without hesitation she went into his arms.

That first touch of his lips was magic.

They were soft, and yet firm, warm and generous, tentative for a moment, then suddenly more urgent. A low growl rumbled in his throat and she leant into him and parted her lips, giving him her mouth.

He took it mercilessly and without hesitation, and she felt her heart slam against her ribs as his tongue plundered the soft, dark depths. He slanted his mouth, his hands coming up to steady her face, and she could feel the uneven thud of his heart and the solid, fascinating pressure of his arousal against her softer thigh.

He shifted one leg between hers and she moaned and arched against him, desperate to eradicate the gap and be even closer—as close as she could be. She felt his hands leave her face and circle her waist, then slide up beneath her T-shirt.

He gave a ragged groan and broke away as he discovered that her breasts were bare, then he lifted her T-shirt and bent his head to suckle her breast.

Her legs nearly collapsed, and at her little cry he lifted his head and his eyes blazed into hers. 'Dear God, Linsey, you're beautiful,' he groaned, and his mouth came down on hers again, ravenous with need.

Time lost all meaning. She threaded her fingers through his hair and pulled him down harder against her mouth, arching into him, her body pleading with his.

And then suddenly, shatteringly, someone cried out his name and he leapt away.

Linsey caught a glimpse of the woman's face, ravaged with shock and pain, and then the woman was turning and running back to her car.

Matthew followed her, calling after her, but she drove away in a scrabble of gravel, leaving the gate hanging open. He stood in the driveway for an age, staring after her, and then slowly, heavily, he closed the gate and came back to Linsey.

Desire had left her now, draining away to leave her cold and sick and shaken.

'Who is she, Matthew?' she asked flatly. 'What is she to you?'

He lifted his shoulders. 'A friend—'

'She's more than a friend! Don't lie to me! I won't

be lied to, Matthew! She looked at me as if she owned you and I had taken you away from her. She looked at me as if I had killed her inside. I want to know, Matthew. I want to know who she is, and what you've said or done that gives her the right to look at me like that.'

'What the hell makes you think you've got the right to ask?' he snapped.

'That kiss,' she said bluntly.

After a moment his shoulders dropped. 'I'm sorry; you're right. I had no business kissing you like that.'

'Obviously not. Your mystery visitor would certainly agree.'

He sighed and rammed his hand through his dishevelled hair. 'Her name's Jan. We've been going out together off and on over the summer.'

'Are you sleeping with her?'

His head snapped up. 'What business is it of yours?' he asked furiously.

'Business? I'll tell you what business it is! You weren't about to stop kissing me there, Matthew, and I wasn't about to stop you, either. That kiss was going all the way, and we both know it. So tell me, and stop beating around the bush.'

She stared him down, and after a minute he turned away, his eyes closing. He had the grace to look ashamed. 'No, I'm not sleeping with her,' he said heavily. 'It's never become that serious—'

'She looked pretty damn serious.'

He sighed. 'Yes. I think perhaps she is. I hadn't realised. Look, I ought to go and talk to her.'

'Yes, I think you should,' Linsey said shortly. 'You've got some fence-mending to do and, judging by the look on her face, it's going to take some pretty fancy footwork to get you out of the mire you're in. You'd better take me home.'

She stalked out of the door, walked to the gate and held it open. The drive back was accomplished in silence, and, having seen her in, Matthew drove rapidly away in the direction of Lymington.

She didn't envy him one little bit, but it was his own fault. He had no business philandering with her if there was another woman on the scene. She went up to her flat, made a cup of tea, sat curled in the big chair that Matthew had sat in earlier and reflected on how their evening would have ended if Jan hadn't turned up.

In bed, without a doubt—unless they hadn't even made it that far. They had both been well past the point of reason.

And that was another thing. If he wasn't sleeping with Jan, then it seemed unlikely that he would have a supply of condoms to hand, and Linsey certainly didn't carry anything like that round with her. For the past few years at least, she had been too busy to hold down a relationship, and with the exception of this evening's regrettable lapse she had never found herself wanting to go to bed with anyone without knowing him very well first.

It seemed, then, that Jan might have done her a favour by turning up out of the blue. She didn't feel grateful, though—far from it. She sipped her tea, closed her eyes and groaned softly. She could still feel his lips, and the moist velvet sweep of his tongue—

She whimpered with frustration. Her body still throbbed with longing, and she was racked with a fierce urge to wrap herself around him and draw him into herself, both physically and spiritually.

She catapulted out of the chair, dumped the mug on the table and changed into her jogging gear. Damn and blast the man, she would run off the frustration.

She let herself out and jogged down the road to the high street, then down to the sea front and along the beach. It was quiet now; the trippers had mostly gone home, and apart from the odd person walking a dog she was alone. She ran to the end of the prom, then turned and ran back inland, cutting across the park and then down and back along the leafy street to the practice.

There was a light on, she saw to her dismay. Not Matthew, she thought; please, not Matthew. But it was Tim, calling in to collect some notes before a visit.

'Hi,' he said cheerily. 'That looks very healthy.'

She laughed, leaning against the reception counter and taking her pulse. A hundred and sixty-two. Fine. She let it settle and chatted to Tim for a moment.

Then she heard a door open behind her and her heartbeat picked up again. 'Linsey?'

She turned and looked at him. He looked grim, and, softy that she was, she felt sorry for him.

'Can I have a word with you?'

'Sure. See you, Tim.'

She went past Matthew, up the stairs to her flat. He followed slowly—reluctantly?

'Where have you been?' he asked, his eyes scanning her shorts and vest-top.

'Jogging. Why?'

He shrugged. 'Just wondered.' His eyes swept up and locked with hers. 'I saw Jan.'

She looked closely at him, at the faint red imprint of a hand on his cheek. 'I see you did. I gather she was unimpressed.'

'You might say that.' He sighed and ran a hand through his hair, pacing across her sitting room to stand at the window, staring out at the darkening sky. 'I shouldn't have done what I did. Whether she'd seen us or not, I shouldn't have done it. I hope you'll believe me if I tell you that I didn't take you back there with the intention of making love to you.'

'I invited myself.'

'I could have said no. Even when we arrived, I had no intention of doing what I did.'

'Kissing me?'

'Making love to you.'

'Is that what you were doing?'

'Oh, yes,' he said softly, turning towards her. 'You know that.'

Her heart thumped again.

'I just want you to know I won't do it again.'

She nodded, perversely disappointed. 'OK. Will you be able to patch things up with Jan?'

He shook his head. 'No. She's made it clear she doesn't want to see me again. We had a long chat. She's been feeling discontented with our relationship for some time, apparently, but she's never said anything.' He sighed again and turned back to the window. 'That's the second time, you know.'

She frowned, not understanding. 'The second time that what?'

'That my obsession with you has messed up a relationship.'

She found that very interesting. 'Obsession?' she said carefully.

'Obsession. After I fished you out of the river I couldn't get you out of my mind. I kept dreaming about you falling in and not being able to find you under the water. Sometimes I'd find you but I couldn't pull you free. Always, before you fell, you turned your head and looked at me, and I started to walk towards you.'

He laughed bitterly. 'I made the mistake of telling Sara about it. She was highly unimpressed—so unimpressed, in fact, that she walked out a little while later.'

'But you couldn't help your dreams!' Linsey protested, appalled that she could have ruined his life all those years ago. She knew about the dreams—oh, yes. All about them. 'You had no control over them.'

He gave a little grunt of laughter. 'No—but she didn't have to like it. Ah, well, it might never have worked anyway.'

'And Jan?'

He smiled without humour. 'Ah, yes, Jan. I was going to ask her to marry me.'

'And yet you could kiss me like that?' Linsey said in disbelief.

'Apparently. I never kissed her like that, you know. Not even remotely. I never wanted to.'

'But you wanted to kiss me.'

His eyes locked with hers. 'Yes. I wanted to kiss you. I still do, but I won't.'

She took a steadying breath. 'Do you want me to go?'

He was silent for a long time, then shook his head. 'No. It won't do any good. My relationship with Jan has been shown for what it is, and with Rhys off we need all the help we can get. You going won't help solve anything at all.'

'I just thought, if it was what you wanted. . .'

'You know what I want. I want to take that vest-top and peel it over your head, and strip those shorts off you inch by inch, and then put you in the shower and get in with you and wash every inch of you. Then I want to lift you out and dry you, and take you to bed and make love to you until you can't stand up for a fortnight.

'But I won't,' he added, 'because that wouldn't solve

anything either. So we'll work together, side by side, and I'll give you tutorials, and we'll be good kids and keep our hands to ourselves, and if we get really lucky we'll manage to sleep for a few minutes every night without being racked by lust. How does that sound?'

She almost said, Tedious, but thought better of it. 'We'll give it a try,' she said instead.

'It'll work, Linsey,' he vowed. 'It has to, because I've got to go on with my life, and I can't allow you to mess it up again.'

It was almost hurtful the way he said that. She could have told him that for years she hadn't been able to kiss anyone with her eyes open because their eyes had been the wrong colour. She could have told him that her two affairs had been boring and awful, and in the throes of the nearest that she had ever come to ecstasy she hadn't felt one tenth of what she had felt with him that evening.

She didn't, though. She simply said, 'I'm sorry.' And she was. She knew the impact she was having on his life. It was entirely mutual—and unbelievably difficult to live with.

Suddenly a year seemed a long, long time. . .

CHAPTER FIVE

BEING flung in at the deep end was often the best way to learn a job, Linsey thought. It was also the most tiring. Despite the fraught and difficult evening that she had had with Matthew, Linsey fell into bed that night and slept dreamlessly until six.

Then she got up and padded downstairs to the surgery, switched off the burglar alarm and settled down in her consulting room with a cup of coffee and the morning's notes. There were one or two patients whom she was a bit concerned about and would have liked to consult Rhys on, but she didn't like to disturb him. She didn't feel she knew him well enough to intrude on his personal problems, and Matthew could probably answer the questions.

She chewed the end of her pen and flicked through the rest of the notes—no problems. So there were just the two; the man who had had an operation for cancer of the prostate some months before, and a young woman whom Rhys was investigating for Crohn's disease, a serious bowel disorder.

She decided to shower and dress and then perhaps phone Matthew and ask him to come in early to go over them with her; she was halfway up the stairs when she heard her own phone ringing.

She ran up and answered it on the fourth ring, and was surprised to hear Rhys's voice.

'Hi,' she said, and wondered what she was supposed to know.

'Hi. Look, Linsey, I'm sorry I woke you but I was a bit worried about a couple of my patients.'

She smiled. 'You didn't wake me. I was downstairs looking at the notes a minute ago. Why don't you go first? And then I'll ask you about the two I'm concerned about.'

'OK,' he agreed, sounding relieved. 'The main one is a woman who's presented with symptoms of severe haemolytic anaemia. The thing is, I've been turning it over in my mind and there's something I can't get hold of. Could you dig out her notes and perhaps even get her back in and check up on her? Her name's Nana Dickenson—Suzanne will know her. There must be something I've missed, but I'm damned if I know what it is.'

Linsey scribbled the name down, then asked about the other patient.

'Oh, Mrs Carter. I think she's got Crohn's. Would you ask Matthew to look at her?'

'Sure—she was one of my queries. The other's Mr Joiner—he was referred for CA prostate and he's come back. You don't know what for, I suppose?'

Rhys didn't. 'Watch out for bone pain. That's the most common site for metastases—primarily the hip, spine and ribs. He's also had heart problems in the past which might be playing up again—the heat might be getting to him. If it's insidious, give it to him straight. He's very acute and won't miss a trick, and if you try and bamboozle him he'll immediately assume he's got a fortnight left to live.'

'OK,' she said, feeling far from OK. She really felt that news such as that should be conveyed by someone who knew the patient, but that was ridiculous. He might have an ingrowing toenail! She would have to play it by ear.

'Don't feel you have to cope alone,' Rhys said reassuringly. 'Ring me if you're worried. I won't mind at all.'

'I will.' She bit her lip. She could hardly ignore his situation, and not acknowledging it would be even worse. 'Rhys, I'm sorry about your problems,' she said gently.

There was a moment's silence when she thought she'd done the wrong thing, then he said, 'Thanks,' gruffly and cleared his throat. 'I'm very grateful to you for stepping in like this,' he added. 'I'll be back as soon as I can.'

'Don't panic,' she hastened to reassure him. 'I was going crazy watching Matthew work while I twiddled my thumbs. Please don't rush back on my account!'

He chuckled, just barely, but it was a chuckle nevertheless. 'Thanks, Linsey. You're a star. I'll take you out to dinner when I've got everything settled here—to say thank you.'

'You don't have to thank me—' she protested, but he cut her off.

'I do. You can have no idea how much it helps to know the practice isn't in the lurch— Oh, blast, Mark's woken up. They couldn't sleep last night, the older two. They don't understand.' He laughed bleakly. 'Damn it, I don't understand. I have to go. I'll be here most of the day. Remember, ring if you've got a problem.'

'I will. Thanks, Rhys.'

She cradled the phone gently. Poor man. He sounded exhausted. He probably had hardly slept all night, if at all.

She showered, dressed and breakfasted, then went downstairs again and jotted pencil notes against Mr

Joiner and Mrs Carter. She'd get Suzanne to deal with
Mrs Dickenson, and in the meantime she'd check the
notes and see what pathology had turned up—probably
nothing but there was no harm in looking.

Matthew knocked and came in just as she was getting
ready to start her surgery.

'Hi,' he murmured.

She met his eyes, then her own skittered away. She
didn't want to remember that kiss—especially if there
wasn't going to be another one.

'Hi,' she replied.

'Any problems?'

She shook her head. 'I've spoken to Rhys—he rang
at seven-thirty.'

'How was he?'

She sighed. 'He sounded pretty rough, really. I tried
to assure him I could cope, but I don't know if he
believed me.'

'You don't have to,' Matthew reminded her. 'I'm just
next door if you start to disappear without trace.'

She smiled at him, and her heart thudded at the
answering quirk to his lips. Damn and blast, why did
she find the man so attractive?

'By the way, can you tell the patients if they ask that
Rhys is away for personal reasons? Don't go into details,
but don't say he's on holiday, either, because he had a
fortnight in June and they get uppity if we're seen to be
enjoying ourselves.'

His grin was infectious and did incredible things to
his eyes and her blood pressure. She sighed as he closed
the door, then she pressed the buzzer for her first patient.
Please God let it be straightforward. After that smile she
was going to have trouble concentrating on her
own name!

Her surgery was fairly uneventful in the end, except that, as Rhys had suggested might be the case, Mr Joiner was complaining of backache. He had no previous history, and Linsey's suspicions were immediately aroused.

'When are you seeing your consultant again?' she asked him.

'Tomorrow, as it happens,' he said. 'Why?'

'I'd like you to mention it to him. He can arrange X-rays as he's on the spot, and it might have some relevance to your treatment.'

His face clouded. 'You mean secondaries.'

She put her pen down and met his eyes. 'There is a slight possibility, yes,' she agreed gently. 'However, there's no need to be concerned at this stage. He'll arrange an X-ray and will discuss the result with you. It's much more likely to be a touch of arthritis or just good old back trouble, but I feel we should eliminate the possibility of anything more serious.'

He shook his head. 'No. I had a feeling it was this. I'll see him tomorrow and we'll go from there, but I had a feeling.'

'Of course, if it is, and I'm not saying it is, catching it early with radiotherapy can make a huge difference.'

He smiled gently at her. 'Don't try to soften it. I know it's curtains. I'm sixty-seven. I've had a good life. I'd rather go now, quickly, than linger on to ninety-seven like my old grandfather. He was blind, deaf and helpless for ten years before he died. Terrible. No, my dear, I don't want a lengthy prison sentence. I'd rather have the electric chair.'

He stood up stiffly and smiled at her once again, and then left, a stick and his pride holding him upright.

She filled in his notes, saw the last two patients and went out to Reception.

'April, could you do me a favour and check up on Mrs Dickenson, please?'

'Nana? Sure. She's not looking too good, you know.'

'Yes, I gathered. Have we had a blood-test result?'

April called the patient's records up on the screen, scrolled through the notes and nodded. 'Yes. Haemolytic anaemia. Red cell count is recorded as very low. Here, have a look.'

Linsey scanned the screen and pursed her lips. 'Wow. I think we'd better arrange for her admission to Lymington Hospital for a blood transfusion, just to be on the safe side, and I need to look in the textbooks.'

She pulled out a haematology reference book from the shelf and sat with it open at haemolytic anaemia, waiting for divine inspiration to strike.

It didn't. She shouldn't have been surprised.

Tim came out of his surgery, grabbed the notes of his visits and left. He had no ideas.

'I've put you down for the emergency surgery, by the way,' April warned her. 'The first patient will be here in a minute.'

'Fine,' Linsey mumbled. She was scanning the notes, and nothing made any sense.

Matthew came and added his two-penn'orth, but they still got nowhere. Then Suzanne came out of her office.

'Who are you talking about?' she asked.

'Nana Dickenson.'

'Oh, I know. Husband Tiny owns the kebab house. Well, not her husband, really. She's divorced—lives with him. They've got three children. She's Greek.'

Matthew and Linsey turned to each other and smiled. 'Favism,' they said together.

'What?' April said with a frown.

'Favism. It's peculiar to areas of the Mediterranean.

They have a fairly common genetic condition known as G6PD deficiency, and basically they're missing an enzyme that protects the red cells from attack by certain chemicals. In the case of affected Greeks, it's the chemical contained in broad beans—fava beans is the other name for them, hence the name favism.'

'So all she needs to do is have a blood transfusion, and make sure she doesn't ever eat broad beans again. And her children shouldn't either,' Matthew said with satisfaction.

'I doubt if they would,' April said, wrinkling her nose. 'Broad beans are disgusting! No self-respecting kid would eat them.'

'I'd better check. Could I have her phone number?'

She rang Mrs Dickenson and asked her if she'd eaten broad beans recently, and was told that yes, she had. Bingo! Arrangements were made for her to go to hospital for a transfusion, and then Linsey hung up.

'Are you coping?' Matthew asked her softly.

'Oh, yes. I've cured a woman of a life-threatening disease and condemned a man to death. Things are just peachy.'

His smile was gentle. 'That's general practice for you, Linsey. How about a tutorial tonight, after surgery?'

'You're on duty,' April reminded him.

He groaned. 'Right, well, how about coming out with me now on my rounds and we can do it as I drive?'

'I've got the emergency surgery.'

He looked at April. 'How many?'

'Three.'

'I'll share them. Are they here yet?'

'Two are.'

He winked at Linsey and stood up. 'Come on, Dr Wheeler. Hi-ho, hi-ho.'

The emergency case she saw was quickly and easily dealt with: a child with obvious otitis media, a middle ear infection that was making him vomit, giving him a raised temperature and generally making him feel thoroughly unwell. The eardrum was still intact but quite inflamed, and she prescribed an antibiotic syrup for the little lad, handed the scrip to his mother and sent them on their way.

Now for the last one, she thought, only to find that Matthew had taken the third patient already and she was free.

He came out a few moments later, bag in hand, and they left promptly.

'Tell me about your surgery,' he said as he turned the car out of the drive and headed for the first call.

'Oh, it was pretty much of a non-event except for Mr Joiner and his back pain.'

'Yes, I'm afraid that's probably not good news,' he agreed. 'We might be wrong.'

'And pigs fly,' she said heavily. 'He said he'd rather have the electric chair than a lengthy prison sentence.'

'Let's just hope he doesn't end up on death row for years. Lots of cancer sufferers do exactly that.'

'Maybe he'll be lucky one way or the other.'

'Maybe.'

Matthew handed her a stack of notes. 'Here. The first call is to Mrs Simms—you remember we saw her at the hospital yesterday. I want to make sure she's all right. Then there's a routine visit to an elderly man who can't make it to the surgery. He's finding the heat a bit much at the moment, according to his son. We'll see if there's any need to admit him. Then Mrs Arkwright, who's booked for a hip replacement tomorrow and just wants to chat about it.'

'And you'll visit her, just for that?' Linsey asked, incredulous.

'Of course. She's housebound, scared to death and I can reassure her and take away some of that fear. That's why I'm here. Why are you here?'

She smiled. 'I just didn't realise there was still time to reassure. In hospital it's all so fast—in, out, ten minutes for this procedure, five for that, forty minutes for another. You lose touch with what it's all about.'

Matthew's laugh was wry. 'Believe me, it's easy to lose touch in general practice, too. Anyway, I want to make sure she's fit enough before she goes in. There's no point in unsettling her if the anaesthetist is going to find she's unfit at the starting line.'

Mrs Simms was well enough, happy to be back in her own home, and although she was still very breathless when she arrived at the door Matthew assured Linsey that for Mrs Simms that was quite normal.

'She's not very well, is she?' Linsey said thoughtfully as they left.

'No, but a lot of our elderly patients aren't.'

'How can she cope at home alone?'

He shrugged. 'She can't. She has help with shopping and meals on wheels and she has a home help from social services once a week, but otherwise she muddles along. We keep an eye on her and others like her.'

So he was an old softy too, Linsey thought, and smiled inwardly. That was what continuity did for you, of course.

Mr Briggs, the elderly man with arrhythmias who was suffering with the heat, was another case. He lived with his son, and so Matthew left him there with oxygen and instructions to the son to buy him a fan and close curtains and open windows to let the air circulate but keep the sun out, and to call if there was any deterioration in his condition or if he complained of any chest pain.

'Why didn't you admit him?' she asked.

'Because he gets very confused if he goes anywhere different, and when he comes home he's often incontinent. He goes into Milhaven every now and then for respite care so that his family can have some time off, and when he comes out the stress is much worse. They told me last time they don't think they'll bother again.'

'Could they get a carer to come in so they can go away?'

'I don't think so,' he said with a shake of his head. 'Financial pressures. The old boy hasn't got any money, and his son's job isn't any great shakes. It's the daughter-in-law I feel sorry for. She's trapped there with a man she's not even related to who is terminally difficult to get on with, and she's getting carer's syndrome. It's a worry. I can tell you, after what I've seen I'd never live with my children.'

She shot him a laughing look. 'What children? Is there something else you're not telling me?'

He grinned. 'Figure of speech. If I get like that they're better off unborn.'

'What do you mean, if? You're surely difficult enough now, aren't you?' she teased.

'How did I end up with you?' he asked, pretending to be affronted. 'Legs with attitude.'

She spluttered with laughter. 'I am not.'

'You are. Right, here's Mrs Arkwright's house. We'll go and explain about her hip replacement, and then we'll head back to the surgery.'

It was a small bungalow beginning to show signs of neglect, and Linsey guessed that the owner was gradually becoming less and less able to deal with it. Matthew rang the bell and Mrs Arkwright opened the door after an age.

'Oh, Doctor! How good of you to come. Do come in,' she said in a remarkably firm voice, and hobbled back towards her chair, leaning heavily on her walking frame.

She dropped into the chair with a grimace of pain, and then carefully put her leg up on a stool and lay back, wincing. 'Oh, dear. Just give me a moment,' she said.

'They're not doing it before time, are they?' Linsey murmured.

'Absolutely not. Better now, Mrs Arkwright? I understand you're having your op tomorrow.'

'That's right,' she said. 'And I have to say it's not a moment too soon.'

'No. How have you been since I saw you last?'

'Very well. I know everybody else is complaining about the heat, but frankly it suits me. All those years in India must have conditioned me, I suppose, but I find I can cope with the heat and my leg hurts so much less.'

'Let me just have a listen to your chest and take your blood pressure while I'm here, can I? Then I'll be able to send you off with a clean bill of health.'

Linsey watched as he checked their patient over and declared her fit as a flea and ready for anything.

'So, what will they do, again? I'm sorry to be such a nuisance but I do worry about it. How will I cope afterwards?'

'You'll be fine. First of all they'll admit you and check you over, just as I have, and then they'll draw on your hip to make sure they operate on the right one, and take you down to Theatre. The operation takes about an hour, and then you'll wake up back in your bed feeling probably a lot better than you have for ages.'

She chuckled. 'I hope so. Oh, I do hope so. So, what exactly do they do?'

Matthew whipped out a pad of paper and sketched a thigh bone and the hip joint, and explained where the bone would be cut, the new ball fitted on the end and the new socket cemented into place, and he showed her where she would have stitches and how long the incision was likely to be.

'You'll be walking easily within a week, and home as soon as you can get about with sticks. You'll have to be careful not to bend too far and not to turn that leg certain ways—they'll show you that. It's just that the joint support is a bit fragile for a month or so and has to have time to heal. Once it has, you should be feeling better than you have for years. Now, who's going to come and look after you at first?'

'I've got a home help coming—one of those carer agencies are sending a lady to live in for a week. I thought it made sense.'

Matthew agreed, and after a few more moments they let themselves out. They were just pulling away when the mobile phone warbled.

Linsey answered it. It was April at the surgery, sounding a bit flustered.

'There's a young woman here who wants to see a woman doctor—she seems quite shaken up but she's adamant it has to be a woman, and Rosie Farmer's on her half-day. I wonder if you could come back, Dr Wheeler?'

'I'll check. Hang on.' She turned to Matthew and repeated the message, and a quick frown creased his brow.

'Does she say what it's about?'

Linsey checked. 'No. No idea, but she's looking distressed.'

Matthew sighed, checked the mirror and spun the wheel. 'Tell her we're coming back. So much for that nice pub lunch I had in mind!'

'I'm Linsey Wheeler. Won't you come in and sit down?'

The young woman came into the consulting room, her eyes wide and watchful. She perched on the edge of the chair and looked as if she was about to run away. Her knuckles were white where she was gripping her handbag and Linsey could see that she was very badly traumatised. She looked clean—too clean. Scrubbed.

Linsey had a very bad feeling.

'Will you tell me your name?' she probed gently.

Grey eyes turned to her. 'Clare,' she said in a harsh whisper.

Linsey nodded. It was a start. There had been no hesitation, so she was confident it was the woman's real name. 'Can you tell me what's happened to frighten you, Clare?'

Her mouth opened, but no sound came out. Linsey could see her casting around for the words, but nothing seemed to be able to make it past her lips.

Finally her eyes closed and she let out a shuddering sigh. 'It was awful,' she whispered. 'He followed me. I was going home—about midnight. I had to get my car from the car park. I heard these footsteps getting closer, and then he just—'

She broke off, biting her knuckle. Linsey gave her time, then prodded again gently. 'What, Clare? What did he do?'

'He dragged me into the bushes, and he— Oh, God, it was sick. He was so foul—I'll never be clean again—'

She broke down, her shoulders convulsing, but no sound came out. Linsey crouched beside her and put her arms gently round her. 'Shh, Clare, you're safe. It's all right.'

The woman lifted her head. 'But I'm not! How do I know I haven't caught something really awful?'

Linsey moved back to her chair but kept her hand on Clare's. 'Clare, did he rape you?'

Her eyes squeezed shut and she shuddered, then nodded slightly. 'It was disgusting. I can't get the smell of him off me. . .'

Linsey squeezed her hand. 'Have you been to the police?'

Her eyes widened and she snatched her hand back. 'No! No, I can't. I'll have to see him and testify, and I can't—'

'All right. Clare, it's all right. Will you let me look at you—just to make sure he hasn't damaged you in any way?'

Clare bit her lip, then nodded. 'OK. But just you. No police.'

'All right. But first, would you mind if I talk to a colleague? It's his practice, and I'd like him to know what's going on.'

'He'll call the police.'

'No, he won't. I promise you, he won't.'

'In here, then, so I can be sure he doesn't.'

'All right.' Linsey picked up the phone and asked for Matthew. 'Could you come in for a moment?' she asked him.

Seconds later there was a tap on the door and Matthew came in.

'Dr Jarvis, this is Clare,' she said. 'Clare, do you mind if I tell him what you've told me?'

Clare shook her head, and Linsey ran quickly through

the story, then checked with the shaken girl that she agreed.

Again she nodded.

Matthew leant back against the wall of the surgery, keeping his distance physically so that he didn't frighten her. 'Clare, I know you don't want to go to the police, but I've done some work with them in the past as a police doctor. Now, because I've done this I know the procedure for rape victims, and I know what samples and so on are needed.

'If I were to tell Dr Wheeler what to do, would you allow her to take all those samples? We could send them to the lab with an explanation of what had happened and the information that you didn't want to press charges at the moment, and they could examine the evidence and put it all on file. That way, if you ever changed your mind it wouldn't be too late.'

'Without identifying me?' she said at last.

'Absolutely. We'd tell them only what you permitted us to.'

She chewed her lip, then nodded. 'He might do it again. They might catch him, and he could be punished.' She swallowed. 'Yes, all right.'

'What about the clothes you were wearing last night?' Linsey asked. 'Have you still got them?'

She nodded. 'In the bin. I threw them out. I could keep them, just as they are.'

'Or let us have them. That might be better.'

She nodded again. 'OK. And—can I have an AIDS test?'

'That won't be necessary,' Matthew told her. 'If we can recover a semen sample, then it can be screened for HIV and hepatitis. You won't need a test.'

'Are you sure?'

He nodded. 'Certain.'

'All right.'

Matthew sat at the desk, careful to keep well away from Clare, and wrote Linsey out a comprehensive list of instructions.

Then he left, and she conducted the necessarily very intrusive examination as gently and quickly as she could. There was a lot of bruising all over Clare's body, and Linsey made a note of each bruise, especially those that looked like fingers digging into her arms and thighs. She had a few minor internal lacerations, and as she was already engaged in a sexual relationship with her boyfriend, it indicated to Linsey just how violent an attack it must have been.

She found herself growing more and more angry, and had to force herself to be dispassionate.

Finally the swabs and samples were all collected, including nail scrapings and specimens of Clare's own hair to compare with any that might be found on her clothes.

'We might need a sample from your boyfriend if you've had intercourse recently, to differentiate,' Linsey told her, but Clare's eyes widened.

'No! I can't tell him! He mustn't know! He'll say I'm dirty—'

Linsey let her cry for a while, then gave her a little hug. 'Fancy a cup of tea?' she offered gently.

Clare nodded. 'I'm taking a lot of your time.'

'That's all right. I'll leave you to get your things back on while I make the tea. In fact, if I give you some paper and a pen, why don't you sit and write down everything you can remember—about him, the place, the nature of the assault—anything at all—and then sign it, so that if you decide to press charges you've got it all written down while it was fresh?

'And,' she added, 'you might also find it helps you to work it all out of your system if you put it down on paper. Try it. It always works for me if I'm really upset about anything.'

She left Clare dressing and went into the kitchen. Matthew was there. He pushed a cup of tea towards her.

'OK?' he asked.

'She may be, one day. What a bastard. I was going to take her a cuppa.'

'I'll make some fresh. Get all the samples?'

She nodded. 'She had internal lacerations. What kind of a brute was he?'

'Where do you want me to start?' Matthew said flatly. She could tell by the very lack of expression that he was as angry as she, and it was comforting.

'Do you think she'll go to the police?' Linsey asked him.

'I have my doubts. It's traumatic enough without having to go over it again and again to the pedantic satisfaction of the judicial system.'

'But he won't be caught unless she does.'

Matthew shrugged. 'It might be a one-off. It's quite possible it'll never happen again. There hasn't been anything in the news.'

'And perhaps his other victims have also kept quiet,' she said softly.

'Um—can I come in?'

They looked up and saw Clare hovering nervously in the doorway. 'Of course,' Matthew said easily, and stood up, offering her his chair.

He went round the table, made her some tea and pushed it towards her. 'How are you feeling now?'

'Better. I think—perhaps I should go to the police. You could be right. Maybe this is happening to lots of people.' She scooped her long blonde hair back away from her face and Matthew breathed in sharply.

Her neck was bruised—a circular bruise as if the man had tried to strangle her.

'Yes, Clare, I think you should go to the police. The next victim might not be so lucky.'

'What a day.'

Matthew snorted. 'So much for our tutorial session. I'm on duty now—damn.'

Linsey gave a little half-smile. 'I could feed you again—something easy? A stir-fry?'

'Can you be bothered? I could get a take-away.'

She shook her head. 'No. Actually, I'd rather you were here. It's funny, I haven't felt at all worried about being alone in the house at night until now, but suddenly—I don't know. Am I being ridiculous?'

His eyes darkened. 'Linsey, you've got nothing to fear.'

This smile was even smaller. 'Haven't I? A rapist is on the loose, and you say I've got nothing to fear? Tell it to Clare, Matthew. I bet she won't be sleeping peacefully tonight.'

'I'm sorry the session at the police station took so long.'

She shrugged. 'It was hardly your fault. They had to have all the facts. I just hope I managed to get enough DNA material for them to get a positive ID if it happens again.'

'I'm sure you did your best. It isn't easy, especially so long afterwards.'

'Mmm. Come on, let's go and raid my fridge before

the phone rings and you have to go out.'

Matthew switched the phone through to hers and they went up to the flat, and Matthew sat on one of the kitchen chairs, tipped it back and propped his feet on the wall while he watched her.

'She was a pretty girl,' he said idly. 'Looked a bit like you.'

Linsey threw him a sideways grin. 'All blondes look the same.'

'No, they don't. When I was at my obsessive best about you, every time I saw one I looked twice. They never looked quite like you. None of them ever had that certain something that made you stand out from the crowd.'

'I thought,' she said, viciously hacking up onions, 'that you were going to avoid personal issues like that.'

'Like what?'

'Like compliments.'

'That wasn't a compliment,' he said quietly. 'That was the truth.'

She heard the chair legs hit the floor, and then his hands touched her shoulders, turning her.

'God, you're crying!' he exclaimed softly.

She laughed, a little breathlessly. 'It's the onions.'

He took the knife out of her hand, washed her fingers under the tap and wiped her eyes with a dampened corner of the teatowel.

'That's better. I don't want to think I reduce you to tears.'

And then he kissed her.

It was just like before, only better, because she knew what was coming and anticipation added to the excitement.

The stir-fry was forgotten. There was no room in her

mind for anything except sensation, and it swamped her.
The taste of his mouth, the texture of his skin, the soft,
thick mass of his hair between her fingers as she cradled
his head and drew it closer—they combined to drive all
reason from her mind.

She knew only that this was right, that she belonged
to this man and always had, and he belonged to her.
From the first moment when their eyes had met all those
years ago, they had been a part of each other, and she
could no more deny that than she could deny her own
heartbeat.

They moved to the sitting room, sprawling across the
sofa, his weight half on her as his mouth plundered hers.
His hand grazed her side, and she shifted to give him
better access. She felt the warmth of his fingers caress
her breast. They were hard and yet so gentle, cupping
the fullness, his thumb tormenting the aching peak with
soft, teasing strokes. His hips nudged against hers, his
need so obvious and yet so restrained.

'Linsey?' he said softly.

And then the phone rang, shrill and demanding. He
lay motionless against her for a moment, then with a
ragged sigh he rolled away from her and stood up, strid-
ing to the phone.

'Dr Jarvis—yes, hello, Mrs Briggs. Oh, dear. Right,
I'll come straight away. Sit him up near an open window,
and stay with him. I'll be with you in five minutes.'

He turned to Linsey. 'Phone the ambulance—here's
the number and the address. Get them over there PDQ.
It's old Mr Briggs—I think the heat has finally got to
him. Admission to Lymington—could you phone them
as well and warn them? Bless you.'

He handed her her jotter pad, muttered something
about seeing her later and ran.

So much for their second kiss. She rang the ambulance, and the hospital, and then went into the kitchen and shredded up some more vegetables. When he came back—if he came back—she'd quickly fry them with some prawns and noodles. She made a cup of tea and settled down to wait in front of the TV, and tried not to think about the rapist.

Matthew came back after an hour and told her that Mr Briggs had gone into acute left ventricular failure and was touch-and-go. 'That's the trouble with LVF— it can strike so fast, especially in a patient who's already so dodgy. Anyway, he's in. Thanks for ringing round.'

'Have you got time to eat?' she asked.

'How long will it take?'

'Four or five minutes.'

He grinned. 'I've got time.'

He had—just. As he scooped up the last forkful the phone rang, and he was off yet again.

Not quite so fast this time, though. He paused long enough to thank her for the meal, to tell her to set the alarm after him and, if she was worried, just to push the panic button in the flat.

'That'll set off the alarm here and at the police station; or, if you should feel the need to set it off silently, key in the number in reverse and it rings at the police station and my house, without making any noise here. They respond very fast to either method.'

'And do you?'

He grinned. 'Like lightning. Don't worry, Linsey, you'll be all right.' His face sobered and he drew her gently into his arms. 'One day we'll get to finish that kiss undisturbed,' he promised, and, with a gentle brush of his mouth on hers, he left.

CHAPTER SIX

ALL hell seemed to break loose in the practice over the next couple of days. Linsey, remembering her boredom and frustration during the first part of the first day, vowed never again to complain about having too little to do.

Rhys came back on Friday morning, but he was unable to stay the whole day because of a solicitor's appointment.

He looked haggard, Linsey thought sympathetically, and found time to cook him lunch in her flat.

'You're a star,' he said wearily as he cleaned the plate. 'I hadn't realised I was that hungry.'

'When did you last eat?' she asked him.

He looked at her as if she had lost her marbles. 'Eat?' he muttered. 'I have no idea.'

'Oh, Rhys—what about the children?'

He shrugged. 'I've been feeding them—beans and fish fingers and stuff like that. I don't know. I suppose I ought to go and shop but I've got an antenatal clinic this afternoon before I go to the solicitor—'

'I'll do it.'

'But you're taking on enough as it is, Linsey.'

She folded her arms and fixed him with a look. 'Are you saying you don't trust me?' she asked archly.

He laughed. 'Of course I trust you. I'd be delighted if you'd do my clinic. I'll make it up to you one day, I promise.'

She bit the inside of her cheek and hesitated.

'Yes?'

She lifted her shoulders. 'I just thought you ought to know that one or two of your patients seem to have got wind of what's going on.'

He laughed humourlessly. 'I'm sure. What have they said?'

She looked down at her hands. 'One old lady said she was glad Judy had gone and good riddance. You were far too good for her. Another. . . Well, more of the same, really.'

He eyed her sideways. 'Elaborate.'

She did, reluctantly because she didn't like repeating gossip. 'He said it was disgusting the way she'd been carrying on right under your nose, and you deserved better.'

He sighed heavily. 'Oh, well, at least they're on my side. How many said it was no wonder she'd gone off the way I neglected her?'

'No one,' she said honestly and without hesitation. 'No one at all. The only people who have said anything have been one hundred per cent behind you.'

'Of course, if it had been me screwing around I'd be called a randy old dog and I'd get away with it. Not that I mind being the injured party, you understand, but it seems somewhat unfair.'

Linsey was surprised by what seemed like a defence of his wife, and yet his choice of words showed how hurt he had been by her behaviour. 'For what it's worth,' she told him quietly, 'I wouldn't say that at all. I think infidelity in any shape or form by either party is equally unforgivable.'

His smile was wry. 'Oh, innocent, sweet girl. People are the pits. The sooner you learn that, the better. By the way, any news on that rapist?'

She shook her head. 'No, nothing. I hope the girl's

all right. The HIV and hepatitis results were negative, fortunately, so that's one less thing to worry about. I gave her a prescription for the morning-after pill to avoid any unwanted side effects,' she added drily.

'Bastard,' he whispered. 'I'd like five minutes alone with him, or any other spineless pervert who picks on the weak and innocent like that.'

She looked at him, probably six feet four, weighing half as much again as she did, and pitied any spineless pervert unfortunate enough to run into this gentle giant on a dark night. 'Go on,' she said, shooing him out kindly. 'Go and do your shopping—and remember to buy lots of fruit and vegetables.'

'Bully,' he muttered with a grin, and, dropping a kiss on her cheek, he went down the stairs to the surgery.

She watched him go from the window, backing out of his space in the car park as Matthew came in. She waved to Matthew, and he ran up to the flat.

'Hi, gorgeous. How are you?'

She smiled. 'Hi, gorgeous yourself. I'm OK. Want a cup of coffee?'

'Love one— Hey, who have you been entertaining?'

'Rhys.'

Did she imagine it, or did a flicker of jealousy cross his face? She decided to play on it. 'He was hungry and I felt sorry for him. He's rather nice, really. I wonder why she left him? All that sexy muscle and sinew—'

She was yanked hard up against his chest and kissed soundly. 'You,' he said warningly against her lips, 'are asking for trouble.'

'Oh, promises, promises,' she laughed, and with a snort of disgust he dropped her.

She straightened her shirt and smirked at him. 'I've got another antenatal clinic today.'

'Rhys's? I thought he was in.'

'I sent him to the supermarket—he was about to starve the kids to death, I think. He didn't seem to have eaten for days.'

'I'm hungry,' he told her hopefully.

'Beans on toast?'

He nodded. 'Could I? I'll have to go to the supermarket myself and stock up your larder again.' He eased himself down onto a chair and tipped it back. 'I've just come from the hospital, by the way. Mr Briggs died a little while ago.'

Linsey sighed. 'Oh, dear. Still, I suppose the time was right. He didn't seem to have much to live for.'

'He didn't. I think the family will be relieved, and then of course they'll feel guilty because they're glad it's all over. I'll go and visit them later tonight, see if I can help them at all. It's a difficult time, even when it's the right time. Oh, and I saw Mrs Arkwright. She had her op yesterday and she says she already feels much better.'

'Oh, good. It makes you realise how bad it must have been if a major operation brings relief!'

'Oh, absolutely. Some of these hips—when the socket is revealed—look so bad you wonder how the patient's been able to walk at all.' The chair hit the floor as she put the plate in front of him, and he dived into the simple meal as if he was ravenous.

She made some coffee, and sat cradling her cup and watching him eat. There was something satisfying about feeding hungry men, she decided. She'd done more of it this week than she had in a lifetime. In fact, it was rapidly becoming a habit! Matthew was right—they'd almost eaten her out of house and home. She ought to go to the supermarket and stock up.

The antenatal clinic was straightforward fortunately, and so was the evening surgery. She pulled into the supermarket car park and found a space, did her shopping and drove out again. As she did so, she thought she saw someone staring at her, but when she looked round there was no one there.

Odd. She must have imagined it. It was that rapist setting her nerves on edge. Even so, instead of taking her things up to the flat as she unloaded them, she took everything into the rear entrance, closed and locked the door and then ferried the bags upstairs after the alarm was on again and she felt secure.

Matthew was on duty that night, and she felt safe knowing that he was coming and going from the surgery, picking up patient records. She left a note for him where he couldn't miss it.

'Come up and see me some time. L.'

At twelve-fifteen, when she was lying in bed unable to sleep and watching the car headlights track across the ceiling, a set of lights swung through a different arc and she heard Matthew pull up outside, open the back door and turn off the alarm.

He found her note and came straight up, and she greeted him on the landing, dressed only in a mid-thigh-length nightshirt with pussycats all over it. He raised an eyebrow.

'Love the nightie,' he drawled, and smiled gently at her. 'What's the matter, Linsey? Couldn't sleep?'

She shook her head. 'I don't know—I'm probably being neurotic, but I thought somebody was watching me at the supermarket. It just unsettled me.'

'Do you want me to stay here tonight? I'll sleep on the sofa.'

'You could sleep in my bed,' she said softly.

His eyes darkened. 'My God, girl, you pick your moments. I've got three calls to make. They're coming in clusters tonight.'

'Can I come with you?'

'Of course. Don't you mind?'

She shook her head. 'I'd rather do that than stay here alone. I know I'm being ridiculous, but I can't help it. Do you mind the company?'

He hugged her gently. 'Of course not. Go and get dressed and come down. I'll see you in the kitchen.'

She threw on the skirt and T-shirt that she had been wearing earlier, with a cardigan in case the night was cooler, and then ran downstairs. Matthew was ready, and they went out together, setting the alarm.

The calls were fairly straightforward. There was a baby with tummy ache who burped and filled his nappy as they arrived, and immediately settled, another child of four who had been coughing constantly and needed steaming and a course of antibiotics, and a young woman threatening a miscarriage whom Matthew admitted to Southampton for observation.

It was all over and done with by two, and they drove back along the sea front. The phone was mercifully quiet, and Matthew pulled up on the prom and wound down the window. 'Listen to the sea on the shingle,' he murmured. 'I always think it sounds wonderful—so soothing.'

His arm came round her shoulder and he eased her up against him, then one finger tilted her chin gently up to meet his kiss.

'I want you, Linsey,' he said softly against her lips, and then his mouth claimed hers and she was lost. The tender magic of his kiss mingled with the music of the night, and she threaded her fingers through his hair and held him with one hand, the other seeking out the buttons on his shirt.

Her fingers found a gap and slid through, their backs brushing against the satin of his skin. There was a little hair, but not so much that she couldn't feel the warm, supple texture of his skin or the firm underlying muscles that clenched as she smoothed her hand against his chest and inched her fingers lower.

'Let's go back to the flat,' he muttered, pulling reluctantly away, and she unwillingly released him and moved back to her side of the car and fastened her seat belt. Her heart was pounding, her pulse racing.

Finally, it seemed, they were to finish what they'd started on Tuesday night—or so she thought.

However, as they turned off the high street Matthew swore softly. Blue lights flashed in the road, illuminating the front of the surgery. An alarm was sounding, and as they pulled up and got out a policeman with a walkie-talkie approached them. 'Sorry, sir, you can't go in there.'

'Of course I can—I'm the senior partner,' Matthew said shortly. 'What's going on?'

'The alarm went off a few minutes ago, sir. Signs of forced entry at the rear, and the intruder has been through the place. Perhaps you'd be good enough to turn the alarm off and inspect the damage.'

They went round the back, Linsey's heart in her mouth, and went in through the smashed back door, the policeman on their heels. Seconds later the alarm was stifled, and Matthew went through the surgery, looking for damage or anything missing.

'Drugs,' he said shortly. 'The spare stock of drugs is kept in a locked cabinet. It's been forced and the drugs are missing.'

'Which drugs, sir?' the policeman asked.

'I don't know—valium, temazepam, insulin, anti-biotics, painkillers—you name it. I'll get you a complete list off the computer.'

'Right, sir, we'll get onto it right away. And of course we'll need to take your fingerprints so that we can iden-tify the intruder's. Now, if you'd be kind enough to check the other floors?'

They went through the middle floor of the house, where Rhys and Rosie had their surgeries and where the nurses' treatment rooms were situated, and found no further damage. Nothing had been moved or touched in her flat, and so it was decided to board up the door and leave the alarm on again for the rest of the night.

'You'll come home with me,' Matthew told Linsey, to her relief. Romance was far from both their minds. All Linsey could think about was how close she had come to being there when the burglar had broken in, and how glad she was that Matthew had been on call. She imagined that his thoughts were on the same lines, and when they arrived at his cottage she went upstairs and into his spare bed without a murmur.

'Rise and shine.'

She opened bleary eyes to find Matthew standing over her, a steaming mug in his hand. The sun was shining, the birds were singing and the break-in seemed light years away.

She scooted up the bed, heavily conscious of Matthew's soft, worn T-shirt that she had borrowed last night. 'Thanks,' she said huskily, her voice unused. She sipped the tea, blowing the steam off the top and watch-ing Matthew as he stood at the window.

'The police have been to the surgery again. Their

forensic boys have been through it and got some prints. They need you to check your flat again, but they don't think there's any problem.'

She nodded. 'What's the time?'

'Eleven-thirty.'

'What?' She sat up straight and nearly slopped the tea. 'It can't be!'

His smile was gentle. 'You were shattered. I thought I'd let you sleep. I went in and did the emergency surgery and handed over to Rosie—it's her weekend on. I thought I'd take you back when you're ready.'

'What about the door?' she asked, wondering how she was ever going to manage to sleep there again.

'It's being replaced with a much more secure metal door and frame.'

'But when?'

'Now, as we speak. I've left the workmen there.'

'Oh.' So she would be secure—at least from that angle of attack. There were, of course, all the windows. . . Still, she mustn't be a wimp. Of course she'd be all right. This was a simple burglary, nothing to do with the rapist.

Matthew left her alone and she showered in his bathroom with an amazing power shower that nearly blasted her skin off and left her feeling invigorated and wonderful. Of course she would be all right, she told herself. It was just the accumulation of the rape and the burglary. Neither of them had been directed at her. She must stop being so neurotic.

She dressed quickly in the clothes she had had on last night, and Matthew took her back to her flat. There was a policeman there waiting to speak to her, and she took him up to her flat.

'I wonder if you could tell us if anything's missing from your flat?' he said without preamble. 'We've got several sets of prints from the burglar, and they weren't up here. Yours we've identified—they were all over the place. Also Dr Williams and Dr Jarvis. There were no other fresh prints at all, so we're almost certain that he didn't come up here.'

Linsey felt a wave of relief sweep over her. 'I'm sure nothing's missing. I haven't got anything of any value, and I keep my medical bag in my consulting room. It's still there.'

The policeman nodded. 'Right. Sorry to have troubled you. If you do notice anything amiss during the day, give us a call, but I'm pretty certain you're safe.' He gave her a reassuring smile and left, and she wandered round, picking up a cup and taking it into the kitchen, washing up the glass lying on the draining board— Glass? When had she used a glass?

She shrugged. She was getting neurotic. She went into the bedroom and made the bed, folding and tidying clothes and loading the washing machine. She looked around for her nightie with the cats on, but she couldn't find it. She shrugged again. Probably down behind the head of the bed where she'd flung it. She'd find it later.

Matthew came up and she smiled at him. 'Hi. Door fixed?'

He nodded. 'They've gone. Here's a new key for you. It's got a deadlock and bolts, so you're all secure.'

She took it. 'Thanks,' she murmured. 'Coffee?'

He smiled. 'No. I'm taking you out to lunch. How about the Ship on the quay at Lymington? They do a wonderful steak—and the wickedest puddings.'

She rolled her eyes. 'How did you know?'

He grinned. 'You wouldn't be normal if you didn't have a weakness for wicked things.'

Their eyes met and clashed.

'Like you?' she murmured.

'Hell, Linsey,' he groaned, and then she was in his arms, and they were back to square one. 'Maybe this time,' he murmured, but then the phone rang and he released her with a laugh. 'God clearly doesn't want me to have my evil way with you,' he said wryly, and scooped up the receiver. 'Jarvis.'

He shot her a glance. 'Yes, she's right here. I'll get her for you.' He held the phone out. 'Tricia.'

She took the phone, perching on the arm of the chair. 'Hi! How are you?'

'Never mind me,' Tricia said impatiently. 'Was that him?'

Linsey tilted her head so that she could see him. 'Yes,' she said, 'that was him.'

'Wow, what a voice! Like melted chocolate. No wonder you threw yourself in the river!'

Linsey laughed. 'Yeah, sure.'

'So, how's it going?'

She sighed. 'Oh, fine. We had a burglary at the surgery last night so I spent the rest of the night at Matthew's— and no, we didn't.'

Matthew's eyebrows shot up, and a grin creased his face. Linsey poked her tongue out at him and turned her back.

'Is he still there?' Tricia asked.

'Yes, he's standing on the other side of the room. Why?'

'So you can't tell me whether it's working out OK.'

'Well, I can.'

'I'll ask. Has it been difficult?'

'No, not really.'

'Is he as gorgeous as you thought? What about his wife?'

'Uh-uh.'

'No wife? He's divorced?'

'No.'

'Widowed?'

'No.'

'Single—he sounds like *that* and he's still single? Does he have genital warts or what?'

Linsey laughed helplessly. 'Not as far as I know, but I haven't looked yet.'

'Yet?'

Trust Tricia to pick that up. 'I haven't looked,' she corrected herself.

'Yet.'

'OK. Maybe I will.'

'Be careful,' Tricia cautioned her. 'Not that I don't think it's time you found someone, but you're such a softy you'll get torn to bits by him if you're not careful. Is he just a perennial bachelor?'

Linsey looked at him again. 'No, I don't think so. I think he's just fussy.'

He met her eyes, his own puzzled. 'Are you talking about me?' he demanded.

She nodded and smiled. 'He's looking cross now.'

'You sound terrified,' Tricia said drily.

She laughed again. 'Hardly.'

'So, you've got a really professional trainer/trainee relationship going there, have you?'

Linsey doubled up. 'Oh, absolutely,' she said when she could speak. 'In fact, when he's wearing his trainer's hat he's a demon. Talk about pedantic. He disagrees with everything—'

'*You* disagree, excuse me,' Matthew interrupted. 'You're the most aggravating wench.'

Tricia chuckled. 'I think you've got under his skin, my friend.'

'Hmm,' Linsey said with a twinkle. 'What an interesting thought.'

'I'm coming to see you—I want to know what this man's like and the suspense is killing me.'

'How's your job?'

'Boring. I'm going to switch to general practice. You seem to be having lots of fun.'

Linsey smiled. 'It's a case of hand-picking your trainer. They have to kiss well. I'm off now—Oh!'

Matthew snatched the phone. 'Don't listen to her, Tricia. She is the most unethical, unprofessional colleague I have ever had, not to mention disrespectful. Believe me, that's not the way to get on, and her report will reflect my opinion.'

Linsey laughed again, quite unabashed. His words might be threatening, but he had his arm around her and his hips were pressed up against her side, giving a quite unmistakable message. 'I'm sorry,' he said down the phone. 'She has to go; we're in the middle of a tutorial. I'll get her to ring you back.'

He hung up and turned to her. 'Get your things. You're coming back to my cottage for the weekend.'

Her eyes widened. 'But it's safe now.'

One brow arched. 'Not where you're going.'

A wicked little smile danced in her eyes. 'Oh, really? I'll pack.'

'You do that—and by the way, what haven't you looked for?'

She grinned mischievously at him. 'Genital warts.'

His jaw dropped, and then he laughed like a drain. 'Damn you, Linsey, you deserve everything I'm going to say in that assessment,' he said when he could speak.

She looked innocent. 'It was Tricia's suggestion. She thought that was why you might be single, seeing as you have such a gorgeous voice.'

'I have?'

Linsey shrugged. 'Tricia thought so. Personally I think it's quite ordinary.'

She went into the bedroom and started to pack, then became aware of the slow creak of boards.

The whisper was husky and chilling. 'I'll give you ordinary,' he rasped. 'I am magnificent, and by the time I've finished with you you will be mesmerised for ever!'

A cold shudder ran through her, and her hands came up to cover her face. 'God, Matthew, don't,' she pleaded.

'Linsey?'

His hands cupped her shoulders and turned her into his arms, his voice normal now and filled with remorse. 'Hell, sweetheart, what have I done?'

'Your voice—I don't know,' she mumbled into his shirt. 'Somebody walked over my grave.'

He tutted. 'I'm sorry. Come on, let's get you out of here,' he murmured. 'Grab your things.'

'I can't find my nightie.'

'You won't need it—I'll keep you warm. Let's go.'

They went, first to the Ship on Lymington quay for a delicious lunch eaten outside in the sunshine without a demon or a rapist in sight, and then back to his cottage. They lay in the garden on sun-loungers, in the shade of a little group of birches, and to Linsey's amazement she found she was drowsy.

'Go to sleep,' he told her. 'I'm here.'

Now why should that make a difference? she wondered, and dropped off to sleep.

She woke much later, and, turning towards Matthew, she saw he was sitting up on the side of the lounger and watching her. 'OK?' he murmured.

She nodded. 'Fine. How long have I been asleep?'

He looked at his watch. 'About an hour and a half.'
His smile was indulgent—a rather masculine smile.

'I don't suppose you dropped off at all,' she said
snappily.

He laughed. 'No. I've been gardening. Want a
cold drink?'

She saw the beads of sweat on his brow, and the damp
patch on the front of his T-shirt.

'It's too hot to work.'

He snorted. 'Tell me about it. I've been weeding. Why
is it that during a drought the only things to grow are
the weeds?'

She laughed and stood up, stretching, and his eyes
fastened on the rise of her breasts and he groaned. Slowly
she lowered her arms and met his gaze.

'How about a shower?' she suggested.

'I'll go now,' he said.

'No, us.'

His eyes widened, then his lips parted on a rush of
air. 'What an excellent idea,' he said softly. 'Coming?'

She smiled. 'I hope so.'

'Definitely,' he replied, and took her hand in his. He
was grimy and sweaty, but she didn't give a damn. She
followed him, not that he gave her any choice, and in
the bathroom they peeled off their clothes and went into
the shower together.

The water was wonderful, pounding on their skin,
adding to the excitement—at least, until it ran cold. He
broke their kiss and stepped away, cutting off the water
supply.

'Here.' He wrapped her in a thick, fluffy towel and
picked her up, carrying her through to the bedroom.

'You'll put your back out. There's a lot of me,' she warned.

He snorted and dropped her into the middle of the bed. 'I can cope with you, you gorgeous creature,' he murmured, and began blotting her dry with the towel.

She lay there watching him, her eyes searching every inch of him, fascinated by the texture of his skin, the trailing rivulets of water that zigzagged over his chest and down his abdomen.

She traced one with her finger, right the way down to the soft nest of hair that surrounded his very masculine reaction. His eyes closed and he groaned as her finger trailed on, right to the end, and over, rubbing oh, so gently at the tiny bead of moisture on the very tip.

'No genital warts,' she murmured in satisfaction.

His choked laugh brought her eyes to his face.

'Lord, lady, you know how to ruin a moment,' he grumbled.

Her hand slid back and circled him, stroking gently, and his eyes closed. He shuddered and caught her hand, lifting it to his lips and kissing the palm, running his tongue over it and nipping the pad of her thumb.

'Matthew?'

'Mmm?'

'Take the phone off the hook.'

He reached across to the bedside table, lifted the receiver and dropped it, leaving it to dangle. Then he found a foil packet, ripped it open and handed her the condom.

'Would you?' he asked with a smile in his eyes.

'I might,' she teased, and put it on him with slow deliberation.

He groaned, deep and husky, and then she reached for him, pulling him across her.

The phone dangled, electronic beeps coming from it, and a woman's voice repeating over and over, 'Please hang up and try again.'

They ignored her. Matthew shifted his hips so that he lay above her, poised at her threshold, and kissed her, long and slow and deep. Then he eased into her, giving her time to adjust, and she lifted her hips and took him all.

A shuddering sigh went through her. 'Oh, Matthew,' she whispered, and he shifted slightly, his hand coming between them and touching her oh, so carefully, so softly, so skilfully.

It was like dropping a pebble on a still, silent pond. Her body awoke, ripples spreading out from the centre as he started to move, his body urging her on, his mouth capturing her cries as the ripples reached the banks and she shattered in his arms.

Then he stiffened, crying out her name, and gradually she felt the ripples fade, and the water became still again and silent, waiting for the next pebble to fall. . .

'I've never done this before,' she confessed.

His eyes narrowed. 'Never done what?'

'Made love to someone I don't know.'

He laughed softly. 'Linsey, you know me.'

'I feel as if I do—but then I felt I knew you years ago, and we hardly spoke to each other.'

Matthew's face went still. 'It's irrational. It's just because I saved your life.'

His expression fascinated her. Had he felt the same? His comment had been quiet, but forceful. She made her tone deliberately light. 'The Chinese say you should beware saving someone's life, because you are then responsible for it. Tricia said you're either very brave, extremely foolish or hadn't heard the proverb.'

He snorted. 'Clever girl, your friend Tricia.' His face softened again and he kissed the tip of her nose. 'Getting back to what you said, I'm glad you don't go round jumping into bed with men you don't know.'

'I did with you.'

'You know me well enough. We've spent the week together, for heaven's sake.'

'So how do you explain what almost happened on Tuesday night, before Jan came along?'

His hand strayed possessively to her breast. 'Lust,' he said simply. 'Everyone's entitled to fall off their pedestal every now and again. I guess Tuesday was your day to fall.'

His lips replaced his hand and he nuzzled her breast, licking and nibbling and driving her crazy. She pushed him away. 'Matthew, I'm trying to have a serious conversation here!'

He laughed softly and lay down beside her, his eyes on hers. 'Sorry,' he murmured, looking anything but. 'You were saying?'

'I was saying I don't know you—not well. I don't know anything about your taste in music, or what you read, or what your hobbies are; I don't know what you want from your life, or what you see in me.'

'That's not true. You know a lot about me. You know I share the same values as you, that I like the countryside and solitude, good food, continuity—'

She laughed. 'Yes. And I know you love all your patients, and you give to them far beyond the call of duty. Look at Joe. No wonder he left you this house. I know you're a man he respected. I know your patients and colleagues think the world of you, that the FHSA must think very highly of you if you're a trainer at only thirty-five; I know you have a sense of humour although you try to hide it well.'

She smiled at him and traced the lines around his eyes.

'I also know there's a deeper side of you that you don't share very easily, that you keep still and quiet and private—a side that I can only guess at. That's what I don't know. I don't know why you are as you are.'

'Is that important?'

She ran her finger down his nose, over his lips and down to his chest, dallying with the light scatter of hair. 'I don't know. I would like to know what you see in me.'

His face softened. 'A beautiful, opinionated, self-reliant woman. You fascinate me. You're difficult and awkward, and yet you tease and laugh at me and I want you anyway. You tie me in knots.'

Her hand slid lower, her palm lying flat against the taut planes of his abdomen. The skin there was pale against the darker tan of her hand, and in the hollow of his hip-bone it was unbelievably silk-like. She stroked it, then found herself distracted by his predictable response. Her fingers strayed again, sampling textures, fascinated by the contrast of satin on steel.

His breath eased out on a sigh of pleasure, and she laid her head on his chest and watched her hand torment him. A little bead of moisture appeared at the tip, and she moved her head down, her tongue flicking out to capture it.

Matthew thought he was going to die.

She bent over him, her hair like a curtain screening her from view, and her mouth cherished him with infinite care.

He needed her. Know her or not, he needed her, couldn't get her out of his mind, couldn't sleep, couldn't concentrate on anything except her.

Her tongue circled him and then tugged, suckling, taking the breath from his lungs in a gasp of ecstasy.

'Linsey,' he groaned. 'For God's sake, stop.'

She moved over him but he stopped her, the last fragments of his presence of mind focusing on the need to protect her. He handed her a condom in a foil packet and lay back, his lip caught between his teeth, dying as she slowly, teasingly caressed it on.

Then she moved over him again, drawing him into her hot, tight, secret depths. She moaned and rocked against him, and his control shattered. Grasping her hips, he drove into her, again and again, until with a little scream she fell against him, sobbing his name, her body convulsing round him.

He felt the pulsing start deep inside him, then a groan erupted from his throat as the life-force surged from him, leaving him drained.

His arms, weak and almost useless, wrapped around her and drew her still closer, and with a wordless murmur he fell asleep.

Linsey lay against him, feeling the steady beat of his heart against her chest, his arms relaxed against her ribs as he slept. It was too hot but she couldn't bear to move. She belonged here, cradled against his chest, in his arms.

So it was ridiculous. They hardly knew each other.

And yet they belonged together, two sides of a coin, like night and day, darkness and light, fantasy and reality.

She moved at last, easing away from him, taking the condoms and flushing them down the loo, putting the phone back on the hook, picking up their discarded clothes in the bathroom. Heavens, it looked like a scene from a rampant movie, she thought with a very womanly smile.

She ached, her body tender from the unaccustomed attention of a man.

And what a man.

She smiled again. He was a wonderful lover. She had known he would be, at least with her. Their souls called to each other, deny it though he might.

She pulled on his T-shirt and nothing else, and pottered about in the kitchen, clearing up a little and making some tea.

He came up behind her, pulling her into his arms, and she went without a murmur. His hand slid up her thigh and discovered her nakedness, and he groaned.

She laughed throatily and smacked his hand.

'No. Enough.'

'Are you sore?' he asked, nibbling her neck.

'A little.'

'I'm sorry.'

'I'll recover.'

'I'm glad to hear it.' His hand slid up her back, cradling her against his chest. 'You're a beautiful woman, Linsey,' he murmured, and kissed her.

The phone rang. 'Damn,' he muttered, 'I think someone's watching us. Every time I kiss you, that phone rings!'

He picked up the receiver and barked, 'Jarvis.' His face softened.

'Sorry, Rhys. What can I do for you?'

He looked at Linsey, and his face contorted in dismay. 'Yes, of course. No problem. Linsey's here—she can help me. No, Rhys, don't worry. That's fine. Bring them over.'

He put the phone down. 'Rhys has tracked his wife

down. He wants to leave the kids with us overnight and go and talk to her.'

'Oh.'

Matthew's smile was wry. 'Look on the bright side—it'll give your body time to recover before I pounce on you again.'

She laughed. 'I think I'd rather put up with the pain. How many and what sort?'

'Mark, five, Emma, three, and Bibby, who's nearly one.'

She rolled her eyes. 'Terrific. No wonder she left.'

Matthew laughed. 'They're sweet kids.'

'Good. Shall I go and buy some fish fingers?'

He grinned. 'Yes—but I should get dressed first.'

She stuck her tongue out at him, ran upstairs and pulled on some clothes. Three kids for the weekend. So much for romance!

CHAPTER SEVEN

RHYS'S wife was in London, he told them, staying with an old friend. He had tracked her down via another friend, and she had been only too happy to pass on the information. It seemed that Judy's own friends were somewhat disenchanted with the way she had treated Rhys, a fact that Linsey thought spoke volumes.

'Are you sure you'll be all right?' he asked. 'I've written down the number where you can get me, just in case there's a crisis. If you do have a problem, please ring. I can always see Judy another time if necessary.'

'There won't *be* a crisis,' Matthew assured him. 'Just relax and go, and talk to her and forget about the children. They're in safe hands.'

Rhys's smile was strained. 'If you say so. It was you I was worried about, actually, not them. They're being rather demanding at the moment. Their mother's precipitate departure seems to have screwed them up well and truly, especially Mark. He's the worst to deal with. Emma's very quiet, on the other hand, and I'm more worried about her, in fact.'

'And Bibby?'

He smiled tenderly and looked down at the baby perched on his arm, playing with a pen. 'Bibby? Bibby's fine—aren't you, Bibbs? She'll scream blue murder when I go, but she'll settle.'

He handed the baby to Matthew, and immediately she wriggled round and cried, reaching out for her father. He called the two older ones, who were running round the garden like maniacs, and scooped them up for a hug and a kiss.

Mark looked sulky and unhappy, but Emma just clung to her father and had to be prised off. 'I'll be back tomorrow in time for tea,' he assured them. 'Don't worry.'

'Are you bringing Mummy back?' Mark asked, kicking the step with the toe of his trainers.

'I don't think so.'

'Why not?'

Rhys met Linsey's eyes and looked desperate. 'Because I don't think she wants to come back with me.'

'Why not?'

'That's what I'm going to find out,' Rhys said gently. 'I'll tell you when I get back, all right? I must go now.'

Bibby was still crying and holding her arms out for him, and Matthew's attempts to distract her with the pen were failing hopelessly.

'Just go,' he said to Rhys, and Linsey watched the big man's face crumple for a second as he hugged the children yet again, then ran to the car and drove quickly away.

'How about a bath, kids?' Matthew said brightly.

'I don't want a bath,' Mark said with scorn. 'I want to go home.'

'Emma?'

Emma shook her head, and Bibby was still straining after the car and screaming, the pen thrown to the ground.

'How about a bubble bath? I've got a special bath,' he told them. 'It has real bubbles, like blowing through a straw. Want to try? It's like sitting in a fizzy drink.'

Mark looked less anti, but Emma still shook her head.

'It could be pink water,' he said temptingly.

'Really?' This was from Emma, finally looking interested.

Linsey decided they could cope without her. 'I'm going to get supper bought. I'll make something else for us later.'

'Get a bottle of wine,' he said, and she thought she detected a touch of desperation in his voice. She grinned at him over the children's heads, and with a cheeky little wave she escaped.

The supermarket was packed, but she found fish fingers and beans for the kids, ice cream for dessert and some fresh salmon steaks and a bottle of dry white Californian wine for her and Matthew, to eat in the quiet time after the children had gone to bed.

This time nobody was watching her, and she loaded her shopping into the car and headed back to the cottage without a care in the world. OK, so they had the children for the weekend, but Matthew was wonderful, her body was in bliss and nothing could have been better.

She parked in the garden, shut the gate and gathered up the shopping, then walked in through the kitchen door to be greeted by a strange humming noise and a fascinating tide of pale pink bubbles flowing gently down the stairs. It reminded her of nothing so much as a river of lava—

'Oh, my God!' She dropped the shopping and ran to the foot of the stairs. 'Matthew? Matthew!'

He ran out of the bedroom opposite the top of the stairs, skidded on the bubbles and slithered straight down the stairs, coming to rest at her feet in a cloud of pink foam and Anglo-Saxon.

She raised one eyebrow. 'You didn't need to prostrate yourself at my feet. A simple, "Yes, dear," would have done.'

He glowered at her, and she had to bite the inside of her lip to trap the laughter. ' "Casting pearls before swine," I think my mother would have said,' he snapped sharply, and looked around in disbelief. 'What the hell is going on?' he growled, getting very carefully to his feet and wincing.

'I think the children may have found the bubble bath,' she offered.

'Oh, hell,' he muttered, and, turning round, he picked his way cautiously up the waterfall of foam and into the bathroom.

The humming ceased, and moments later there was the sound of water running away.

'It was an accident,' she heard one of the children say. Emma, probably. 'It just fell.'

'I told her not to press it again,' the other one said with deplorable lack of loyalty. Mark.

'No, you didn't!' the little one said indignantly. 'You told me to!'

Linsey followed Matthew carefully up the stairs and went into the bathroom. It was awash, the floor inches deep in pink froth, the children standing naked up to their knees in bubbles, like parasols in a milkshake. Matthew looked at her helplessly.

'I think, children, it would be a very good idea if you just went and put your pyjamas on, don't you?' Linsey said, quietly taking charge. 'Matthew, where's the baby?'

'In the cot, playing,' he told her grimly.

'Right. Off you go, and don't get into any more mischief.'

She shepherded them out of the bathroom, passed them a towel and told them to dry their feet, then turned back to Matthew.

'I suggest we get a dustpan and scoop the foam in here into the bath, then sweep the rest down the stairs and out of the back door.'

He sighed. 'Fine. I'll get a brush and the dustpan.'

'Be careful on the stairs,' she warned him, but the smile must have been lurking in her eyes.

He glowered at her. 'Don't rub it in,' he menaced. 'I am quite sore enough without you adding insult to injury.'

She crouched down and started to feel around for the bath mat. 'You'll probably tread on the toothpaste next. If I were you, I'd swear off anything to do with bathrooms,' she said sagely. 'They don't seem to agree with you— Oh!'

She found herself lying face down in the foam, the sound of Matthew's retreating footsteps echoing on the stairs.

From the doorway behind her came a tiny giggle, quickly stifled, then the sound of the door closing.

She grinned. Wretched kids. She plopped the bath mat in the basin, retrieved a small pair of leather shoes and wondered what else was submerged by the milkshake.

'Are they asleep?'

'Finally.' Linsey flopped down on the sofa, exhausted. 'Have you done anything about supper?'

He shook his head. 'I thought I'd make sure they'd gone off well and truly so they don't get to wreck the salmon as well as the house.'

She smiled tiredly. 'It doesn't look too bad now. How about the carpet?'

'Still very soggy, but I think it'll be all right. It's drying over the bench in the garden.'

Their eyes met, and he patted his knee.

'I'm too heavy.'

'Rubbish. Come here; I want to hold you.'

So she went, and snuggled against his shoulder with a sigh of contentment. 'We can't sleep together, you know—not with the children here,' she told him.

'I know. You have my bed, I'll have the sofa.'

Linsey had a better idea. 'You have your bed. That way, if the children wake up in the night, you get them, not me. And we'd better rig up a stair-gate in case they walk around in their sleep. Disturbed, unhappy children often do.'

'And if they aren't disturbed and unhappy I can't imagine why.'

'Because the mother was a waste of space and Rhys has always been the guiding light in the family?'

'Probably. He's a wonderful father. He's always taken the job very seriously, and he adores them.'

'I wonder how he and Judy are getting on?' Linsey mused.

Matthew sighed. 'Badly. They didn't get on well at the best of times, and this certainly doesn't qualify. I must say, I don't envy her. He's intending to go for custody.'

Linsey nodded. 'Good. He can afford to make sure they're properly cared for, and any woman who dumps her children with a child-minder and goes off because she's fed up, without saying a word to a soul, doesn't deserve to keep her children.'

'Did the diplomatic corps turn you down?' he said mildly.

She refused to laugh. She felt very strongly about it, and although she knew that parents were often under intolerable pressures she still found it difficult to be understanding when the repercussions were always felt by the innocent children.

Well, fairly innocent. She thought of the milkshake bathroom and smiled. 'Fancy a bubble bath?' she said to him.

He chuckled. 'No, and nor do you. I tell you what— after they've gone tomorrow I'll show you what that bath's *really* for.'

'Ooh. Promises.'

'Yeah.' He turned her head and dropped a light kiss on her lips. 'You'd better believe it.'

His hand curved round her hip, easing her against him, and his mouth settled against hers with a sigh. Heat flared between them, and after an age he broke the kiss and rested his head against hers. 'I want to make love to you,' he said huskily.

'I noticed.'

'Damn kids. They're asleep; perhaps we could—'

'No. I wouldn't feel right. Anyway, I'm sore.'

He lifted his head and tipped her chin, searching her face. 'Very?' he asked softly.

She shook her head. 'No, not very. It's been a long time.'

His smile was wry. 'I know the feeling. Oh, well, it's only twenty-four hours.'

She wriggled to her feet. 'How about supper?'

'Good idea. Then I think we ought to get to bed, because they'll be waking up at the crack of dawn, if not before.'

It didn't quite work like that. The theory was fine. The problem was that Linsey, sleeping lightly on the too small sofa downstairs, was the one to hear the thump and the sudden cry as Emma fell out of bed. She cuddled her and tucked her back in, staying there to ensure she settled, and then an hour later she heard the patter of little feet and Mark appeared at the bedroom door.

'I can't sleep,' he told her, and so she took him downstairs and cuddled him up on the sofa under her quilt and told him stories, and gradually he drifted off.

Then the baby cried, and Linsey eased away from the little boy and ran upstairs to comfort Bibby before she woke Emma again. She gave her some warm milk in the kitchen, changed her nappy with a skill she didn't know she had and then rocked her on her lap until she fell asleep. Luckily she managed to sneak the baby back into her cot without her waking and disturbing anyone, and then crept back downstairs, pulled on her clothes and snuggled up in the chair.

Finally at six-thirty she gave up and went into the kitchen and made a cup of tea. Predictably the kettle woke Matthew, and he came downstairs, dressed only in a pair of jeans with the zip yanked up, rubbing his face and smiling sleepily at her.

'Well, they slept all right,' he said cheerfully.

Linsey looked at him disbelievingly. 'You have to be joking,' she muttered, splashing boiling water on the tea.

Matthew came up behind her and put his arms round her as she banged the kettle down.

'Aren't we a morning person, sweetheart?'

She jabbed him in the ribs with her elbow and reached down two cups. 'No, we damn well aren't—not when we've been up all night with someone else's unhappy children.'

His eyes widened. 'What?'

She told him her nocturnal tale of woe, and he hugged her gently and apologised.

'Sit down; I'll make you a cup of tea,' he said consolingly.

'I've made it,' she told him. 'You're too late.'

'I'll pour it. Sit down.'

She sat, grumpy, tired and wondering why Judy had stayed so long. Perhaps it wasn't so difficult after all to understand how someone could just up and leave.

'Have I done something wrong?' he asked quietly, sitting down opposite her.

She sighed. 'No. I was just feeling for Judy.'

'Judy?' His surprise was evident in his voice. 'If you feel for anyone, feel for Rhys. He's been holding together a rotten marriage for two years—or he thought he was.'

'Is Bibby his?' she asked.

Matthew shrugged. 'I would say so. They all look very like each other and like him—the dark hair, the grey eyes. I would think almost inevitably they're all his. Either that or her lovers look like him.'

'Lovers?'

Matthew stirred his tea. 'Lovers. In the plural. I gather it's been going on for some time.'

'Did he know?'

'Not all of it. Not the latest one, and probably not several of the others. Everybody now is in a hurry to tell him all about it, of course.'

'Is he humiliated?'

Matthew shrugged again. 'Possibly. I doubt it. Rhys doesn't have an ego problem. He's more worried about the effect on the children.'

They fell silent, thinking about the children, and as if their thoughts had woken them Mark stumbled out of the sitting room knuckling his eyes and Bibby started to cry.

The bedroom door at the top of the stairs opened and Emma appeared at the makeshift stair-gate. 'Bibby's crying,' she said unnecessarily, 'and I'm hungry.'

*   *   *

Rhys arrived at six, tight-lipped and silent. He hugged the children, his eyes filling, and took them away with hardly a word.

'Whoops,' Matthew said softly.

'Mmm.' Linsey turned to him. 'Now, about that bath. . .'

It was wickedly exciting, made more so by the suspense of the past twenty-four hours. At last Linsey sprawled, slaked, between Matthew's outstretched legs, her head lolling against his chest, and sighed.

'Beats pink bubbles,' she said with a lazy grin.

'Mmm. Definitely X-rated, though.'

She blushed, remembering some of the things they had done, and Matthew chuckled. 'Gone coy on me?'

'In the cold light of day it seems a trifle decadent,' she explained with a sheepish smile.

'Wonderfully so.' He swished water over her exposed breasts and blew on them, watching her nipples peak with the cold. 'Have you ever done a vasectomy?' he asked, idly swishing and blowing in turn.

'No—why? Do you want one?'

'Mmm. It would solve the problem of living with my children in my old age, although if one's kids were truly ghastly to bring up I suppose it would offer a form of divine retribution.'

She turned over to face him, burying her breasts in his groin. 'They were quite a handful, weren't they?'

He rolled his eyes. 'You could say that,' he agreed mildly. 'I suppose it's not so bad if you have them one at a time and get used to it. You must do most of it on autopilot.'

'Especially at three in the morning.'

He hugged her. 'I'm sorry.'

'You'll have to make it up to me, won't you?' she

said with a teasing twinkle in her eye, and rubbed her breasts against him.

His body stirred obligingly, and within moments the children were forgotten. . .

Rhys came back to work the following Tuesday, his child-care arrangements sorted out and the children safe in the care of the new nanny.

She was living in, and was apparently a marvel. Rhys was still tight-lipped on the subject of Judy, but gradually over the course of the week, as the children settled and his work began to fill the hole in his life, he started to unravel a little.

He didn't laugh, though. The fun seemed to have gone out of him, and some days he came in with an obvious hangover.

Linsey worried about him, and she knew that Matthew did too. He spent a lot of time chatting to Rhys in his consulting room, and she hoped he was able to counsel him and help him come to terms with his anger and disappointment.

She didn't think that Rhys was suffering from a broken heart. From what Matthew had said, his love had been killed a long time ago. Still, the sense of failure was the one constant that everyone reported after a marriage breakup, and Rhys was sure to hold himself responsible for having let Judy down, and ask himself why else she would have gone off like that with all those other men.

She remembered what he had said about the rapist, and thought she herself would like five minutes alone with Judy for what she had done to him and the children.

Faithless tramp. Being unable to make a relationship work was one thing. Cheating on your partner was quite another.

The very thought of Matthew with another woman sent a stab of pain through her, and she felt again for Jan, catching them kissing that night at the cottage— heavens, was it only a couple of weeks ago? How had she felt, seeing the man she loved in the arms of another woman? Linsey dreaded to think. And yet, if Jan hadn't come along and they had made love, would Matthew have ended his liaison with Jan?

Yes. She knew that. He wasn't a cheat or a liar. He had just genuinely not realised how involved Jan was with him, but he had made no commitment to her and she had said nothing, so Linsey could absolve him of blame for everything except that of being blindingly unaware of Jan's needs.

Perhaps the other woman should have made them clearer.

Like you are? she thought wryly. Oh, their sex life was wonderful, but what about the emotional side? Did he ever say he loved her?

No. He didn't, but she didn't tell him she loved him either, and if she was being honest she probably should do. She didn't want to overwhelm him, though. She was good at overwhelming people—it was what she did best—and for once in her life she wanted to do things right.

She sighed and picked up her notes. It was no good sitting here after her surgery had finished and hoping that her visits would go away. She was doing them alone now, discussing them with Matthew before and after, consulting with him before referring or admitting when- ever possible, but gradually stretching her apron strings.

He didn't like it. Matthew liked to be in control. Unfortunately so did Linsey, and when she knew she could cope she found conforming to his wishes just the teensiest bit tedious.

Still, he was the boss—at least at work. He was busy with Rhys now, she discovered, so without consulting him she went out on her calls.

The first visit was to Mrs Arkwright, who had had the hip replacement and had been so slow and racked with pain when they had visited before.

This time she opened the door much more quickly, and smiled at Linsey. The lines of strain were still there, but no longer drawn so tight, and she was moving remarkably well.

'How are you?' Linsey asked.

'Oh, Dr Wheeler, I feel fantastic! It's marvellous! I can move around my home again without feeling as if I've run a marathon—I've even been for a walk around my garden! It's marvellous,' she repeated.

She was doing very well, Linsey acknowledged. The wound was healed, the stitches out and there was no sign of infection or any other problem. So long as she was careful not to turn the leg in or bend it too far in case she dislocated the new joint, she would be better in no time.

A life transformed, Linsey thought as she left. A hip replacement was so simple and yet so astonishing in its impact. It was just a tragedy that the waiting lists were so long when every day was agony for those who suffered.

Still, Mrs Arkwright was on the mend.

If only there was such a simple solution for Mr Dean. He was the man who had wanted antibiotics and to whom Matthew had given painkillers when he had a virus. Linsey smiled. They had argued about it, she remembered, and now Mr Dean was demanding a house call and saying he was still quite unwell and needed attention.

She found his house without too much difficulty, and was let in by his wife.

'Oh, Doctor, I'm glad you're here—he's been making such a fuss! He's quite unwell, you know—quite unwell.'

Linsey followed her down the hall into the bedroom at the back of the bungalow, and greeted Mr Dean, who was lying in bed looking fit as a flea but thoroughly sorry for himself. 'Damn painkillers Dr Jarvis gave me did no good at all—stupid man. Don't know what he thought he was doing. Weak as a kitten I am now, and I haven't slept through the night for weeks.'

'Have you been in bed the whole time?' Linsey asked, opening her bag and getting out her stethoscope.

'Of course he has. I've been looking after him very well,' Mrs Dean said indignantly.

'I'm sure you have,' Linsey soothed, sure of nothing of the sort. The wretched man was as well as she was, and was weak because he'd taken to bed.

'I don't like the sound of that chest,' she told him, 'and lying down is the worst thing for it. Obviously you have to go to bed at night, but I think you should have a course of antibiotics and then get yourself up and move around as much as possible. I'm sure you'll notice a great improvement in a few days if you do.'

She scribbled the prescription, shut her bag with a snap and left, smiling benignly. She managed to get into the car and drive round the corner before she allowed herself to laugh.

Matthew was just getting out of his car as she arrived back at the surgery, and she told him about Mr Dean's invalidity.

'And you weakened? You should have just told the idle heap to get his back off the bed and go and dig the garden,' he teased.

'It's not that easy. . .' she began, and then noticed the laughter in his eyes. She hit him.

'Ouch. That'll cost you lunch.'

She raised an eyebrow. 'Really?'

'Really. I'm starving.'

'We could—um—'

Matthew grinned. 'Yes, we could.'

They went in, and found Rhys sitting at the kitchen table, hunched over a cup of coffee.

'Hi, there,' she said cheerfully.

He gave her a morose look. 'Hi. Police rang—they've picked up our burglar.'

'Oh, excellent,' Matthew said. 'That's a relief. You can rest easy in your bed now, Linsey.'

'Whose?' she mouthed.

He winked and jerked his head towards the bottom of her stairs.

Linsey shook her head and then turned to Rhys. 'We were just about to have lunch. Join us?'

He lifted his head. His eyes were slightly bloodshot and he looked grim. 'I don't think so.'

'I do,' she said firmly, and got him by the arm. 'Come on. Tea, toast and a quick zizz on the sofa.'

He went without protest.

'Is he on the bottle?' Linsey asked Matthew a month later as they were trying to fit in one of their tutorials. Rhys had appeared that morning once again looking bloodshot and haggard, and she was worried about him.

'Not on a regular basis, I don't think. Just after another row with Judy or when it all gets too much.'

'Poor man. He doesn't deserve to be so unhappy.'

'We don't know the ins and outs of it, Linsey. Maybe he didn't give her what she needed.'

'No—and maybe she didn't ask. He's not psychic.'

Matthew looked at her. 'Nor am I. What do you need from me?'

She hesitated. What if she said commitment? Would he run a mile? Probably. 'How about a tutorial?' she said lightly.

He looked at her searchingly. 'Fine. What do you want to talk about?'

She scraped around in her mind for something sufficiently distracting and unromantic. 'Tell me about your endoscopy sessions and gastrointestinal screening programme.'

Matthew walked slowly along the sea front, staring out over the sparkling water at the endless little boats zipping back and forth across the Solent. He could see the Isle of Wight just a few miles away, the Needles clearly visible, marching out into the sea off the point, like lemmings.

He felt like a lemming. The urge to run away was overwhelming him, because he was scared. He was falling for Linsey, and he couldn't seem to do a damn thing about it. Their lovemaking was incredible. Every time, they reached new heights—heights he had never even dreamt of.

She was bold, too—bold and beautiful and often dominant, as diametrically opposed to the girl of his fantasies as it was possible to be. All those years ago, when she had haunted his dreams, she had been meek and submissive and wide-eyed, adoring and virginal.

The real Linsey was aggressively sexual, and

delighted in his body and her own. He was a little shocked sometimes by her frankness, but he wouldn't have changed her for the world. The real woman was infinitely more exciting than the fantasy one had been.

The trouble was that he was getting addicted. She was in his blood, under his skin, inside his mind. He was obsessed by her, unable to think about anything except getting her alone and tweaking the hair-trigger of her responses.

She was fitting in well to the practice, too, and he knew he was going to be under pressure soon from the others to offer her the post after the year was up.

Patients were asking for her, Rosie was told a hundred times a week how glad people were that there would be another woman there when she left, and even the men sought her out—a fact that made Matthew seethe with totally irrational jealousy.

She had been with them for nearly two months, and for most of that time they had been together every available moment.

She still slept at the practice, for appearances' sake as much as anything, but nobody thought anything of it if Matthew was there as well, and, with the car park tucked away behind the back, nobody would know anyway.

The cottage they saved for weekends, and as the summer came to a close and the autumn took over they went for walks through the woods behind his house. The trees were ablaze with colour, and as the leaves started to fall and the evenings drew in they spent cosy hours by the fireside.

It was wonderfully romantic—and Matthew was beginning to panic. Every time he got close to a woman something went wrong. Sara had left him; Ellen a few years later had told him that he was boring. Jan had been willing to stay the course, but she'd bored him. Always, it seemed, one or other of the parties got bored. Look at Rhys and Judy, he told himself.

He knew he could never be bored by Linsey. Whatever else she might be, and she was plenty, boring wasn't ever on the cards.

It was by no means out of the question, though, that he would bore her. Once her inquisitive, convoluted little mind had extracted everything it could from their relationship, would she feel trapped? Probably. Bored? Almost certainly. He knew he didn't have the sort of scintillating personality that would be able to hold her. He was quiet, peace-loving, dedicated to his profession. He felt as if he was being sucked along in the slipstream of a magnificent mythical being, and any minute now she would change course and he would fall flat on his face.

Perhaps he should try and cool down, ease away from her, get himself some personal space.

He didn't want it. He wanted Linsey, and with shattering certainty he knew that she had the power to destroy him if she chose to do so.

He had never felt more vulnerable in his life.

Something was wrong. Matthew was quiet and distant, and Linsey, always assailed by self-doubt and unable to see her own worth, wondered if her uncharacteristically aggressive behaviour in the bedroom had shocked and repelled him.

Perhaps he didn't like it when she took the initiative? Oh, OK, physically he seemed more than happy, but was his ego being battered?

She couldn't understand her own behaviour. She was never, ever like this. She couldn't remember ever taking the initiative before—and that wasn't, by any stretch of the imagination, because her experience was so vast that any incident was lost in the mists of time. She just didn't behave like this, and she knew she was frightening him off.

A lump rose in her throat. She needed him desperately. She couldn't imagine life without him, not under any circumstances. Perhaps she should have asked him for commitment when the moment had presented itself, but she knew he'd have made light of it and run screaming.

Damn. She never cried. She wiped the tears off her cheeks angrily and stared out of the window at the glinting sea. Darkness fell earlier these days. Matthew was out, on duty. She was alone, and she didn't want to sit here alone and cry. Knowing her luck, he'd catch her.

She changed into her jogging things and let herself out of the new, supersafe back door that they no longer needed. She'd take the route along the front, up behind the park and home. It took about twenty minutes and she should be back while it was still light if she hurried.

There was a nip in the air down by the sea, and she felt the cool breeze over her heated skin and revelled in it. The summer had been too hot for running, and she was only just now getting back into the swing of it—not that she had had much time, what with Matthew being there every available minute. She'd had plenty of exercise, though.

Warm as she already was, she felt her colour rise at the thought. Lord, she'd turned into such a brazen hussy! She couldn't believe she did some of the things she did. Last week she'd covered him in honey—covered, mind you—and licked it off, inch by glorious inch.

She'd felt sick later, but it had been worth it.

She turned up by the park and pushed herself. It was

darker here, the shadows lengthening, and she didn't like this stretch of road. She always felt as if someone was following her, watching her. Ridiculous. The rapist hadn't struck again, and it seemed likely that he had been a visitor to the area. He was probably long gone. She turned onto the home stretch, powered down the road and turned into the drive with a sigh of relief.

The security lights came on automatically as she ran round the back, and she let herself in, relocked the door and punched her number into the alarm, resetting only the outside doors and the practice.

Then she went slowly upstairs to her flat, peeling off her clothes as she went, and headed straight for the bathroom. She reached for the blind before she turned on the light, and for one terrifying moment she thought she saw someone standing on the other side of the street looking straight at her.

Then a car came down the road, headlights on, and she realised that it had been the shadow of a tree.

She was getting stupid, she told herself. She snapped down the blind, flicked on the light and climbed into the shower. By the time she came out Matthew had swung his car into the car park and was running up the stairs.

His eyes tracked down her body, clad in a little towel that hardly met over her breasts, and the gun-metal turned to molten steel. She smiled and dropped the towel, walking away from him into the bedroom. To hell with playing the mouse, she thought. When he looked at her like that—

She bent over to pick up her clothes and he came up behind her, grasping her by the hips and sliding home without a word.

Her breath caught and she writhed against him, taking him deeper. With a gutteral groan he pushed her onto the bed and thrust home over and over again, his hand coming round to find the sensitive nub that ached for his touch.

She bucked against him, the waves crashing over her, shudders racking her body as the climax ripped through her. Then he fell on her, his body spent, and she laughed weakly.

'Well, hello there,' she said with the last ragged scraps of her breath.

'Hello. Had a good day?'

She chuckled. 'Better towards the end.'

He kissed her shoulder. 'Witch.'

'Any more calls?'

'No.' He eased off her and she turned over.

'Good. How about an early night?'

He hesitated, then a lazy, sexy smile escaped. 'Sounds good.'

That night, while they lay sated in each other's arms, the rapist struck again. . .

CHAPTER EIGHT

THE evening news the next day was full of it. The girl was nineteen, a student, and had been walking home from the bus at ten-thirty after an evening class. She had been brutally raped at knife-point, it was reported, and, thanks to her clear description of the attacker, they were able to say that it was likely to have been the same man who had struck before.

Women were advised not to go out at night alone, to stay in their cars and wait for help if they broke down, and to lock their doors and windows when they were in the house, day or night. It was an extraordinary thing, the reporter said, but the police had remarked how alike both girls were—tall, slim and with striking, long blonde hair.

Linsey's blood ran cold.

So, apparently, did Matthew's. 'That's it,' he said firmly. 'No night calls—neither you nor Rosie. Rhys and Tim and I will cover them.'

'Tim will love that. He and April are just getting it together. I caught them in the treatment room the other day, *in flagrante* or damn nearly.'

Matthew scowled. 'How immoderate. They should have more self-control.'

'What—like we do?' she teased, and he flushed a dull red.

'That's different; we come up here.'

'Mmm. I'm sure they all know.'

'I don't care if they do. It's none of their business.'

'Of course not,' she soothed. 'And I'll be fine doing my visits, so long as I set the alarm religiously.'

'No,' he said emphatically.

'Matthew—'

'No.'

The phone rang and she picked it up. 'Linsey? What's going on down there?'

'Oh, hi, Tricia. What do you mean?'

'This rapist! It sounds horrendous.'

She looked at Matthew. 'Mmm,' she agreed, without giving too much away.

'What do you mean, ''Mmm''? He's targeting people exactly like you, chuck. You watch your step, you hear me?'

'I will. I'm very sensible. I'll be fine.'

There was a distinct and very unladylike snort. 'In a pig's eye,' Tricia muttered. 'You just be careful. What does Matthew think?'

Linsey turned her back on him. 'He's overreacting, just like you.'

'I am not,' he growled, guessing at the topic. 'I just don't want to be responsible for any injury or assault to one of my colleagues—quite apart from any personal feelings I might have on the matter!'

'Yes, and that's the trouble, isn't it?' she snapped, sick of being mollycoddled and controlled. 'You're obsessed by my body, and you can't imagine that every other man isn't too.'

There was a deathly hush, and then Matthew picked up his jacket and walked out without a word.

'Lins?'

She looked at the phone. 'Oh, God, Tricia, what did I just say?'

'Sounds like you just dropped a clanger.'

She chewed her lip. 'I think I did. God, why did I say that? I'm just as obsessed. If tall men with mid-brown hair and gun-metal eyes were being targeted, I'd have him locked up under armed guard so fast he wouldn't know what had hit him.'

'So tell him that. Go and find him and tell him you understand but that he's being over-protective. Tell him you know it's just because he loves you.'

'But I don't know that he does,' Linsey said softly. 'I really don't. I honestly think it is just my body. Every time I open my mouth, we argue.'

'You argue with me too, but I love you. You're my best friend. Just because you're argumentative and opinionated it doesn't stop people loving you, Linsey.'

Her eyes filled. 'Thanks—I think.'

'Go and find him.'

'He's gone.'

'Uh-uh, not with the rapist about. He won't have gone far. I'll bet you he's downstairs. I'll speak to you later— and take care.'

She hung up, and Linsey cradled the receiver and went slowly to the bannisters and looked over.

He was sitting at the bottom of the stairs, hunched over, his elbows on his knees, and he looked prickly and unapproachable. Linsey forced herself to go down and sit beside him.

'I'm sorry,' she said tentatively.

'You're right,' he rasped. 'I am obsessed by you. Obviously I crowd you. I'm sorry; I'll keep out of your way.'

'No!' she cried out, then said, more softly, 'No. You never crowd me. You *never* crowd me. I just hate it when people are over-protective because I'm a woman.'

He turned to her. 'You're vulnerable, Linsey. Look

at yourself.' He picked up a lock of her hair and held it
in front of her eyes. 'You're just like the women he's
raped. I couldn't bear it if it happened to you—'

She went into his arms with a little cry, and he crushed
her against his chest and held her. 'Let me look after
you,' he reasoned. 'Just until they catch him. He's a nut
case. He might have a record—perhaps this time they'll
get something on him.'

'And in the meantime I can't do my job. That's not
fair on you and Tim and Rhys—especially Rhys. And
anyway, Rosie's going any day now so you'll have all
her workload. You can't take on any more.'

'All right,' he said slowly. 'All right, I'll compromise.
We'll leave it as it is, but I'll stay here during the week,
and when I'm on duty you'll have the burglar alarm to
protect you, and when you have to go out I'll come
with you.'

'But you'll be shattered.'

'No. I'll sleep in between the calls. If you're out on
your own ever I won't sleep a wink at all. And you'll
go shopping with me, and running with me—everything.
All right? If you're outside this door between dusk and
dawn, I'm with you. Agreed?'

She tutted. 'Whatever will the neighbours say?' she
teased.

'Damn the neighbours,' he muttered. 'Do you agree?'

'Do I have a choice?'

'No.'

'Then I agree,' she said softly. 'Just for now, and just
to satisfy your honour.'

'Thank you,' he said drily, and stood up, pulling her
to her feet.

She sparkled cheekily at him. 'Don't mention it.'

He sighed and shook his head. 'You are impossible.'

'Mmm. Are you coming back up to the flat, then?'

'What, and be accused of being obsessed with your body? It's true, you know.'

She reached up and smoothed his hair. 'Oh, Matthew, I'm just as obsessed.' Her fingers threaded into the soft, sleek mass and she pulled him down to her mouth.

He groaned against her lips, but his arms came round her and lifted her against him, and only her teasing reminder of where they were and how immoderate it would be stopped him from taking her there on the stairs.

Instead he hoisted her over his shoulder like a fireman and ran upstairs to the flat, dropping her on the bed. 'He-man,' she teased. 'Well, go on, then, finish what you started.'

He undressed her, but slowly, his eyes clouded with some haunting demon, and when he moved over her his kisses, instead of being aggressive and wildly passionate, were tender and protective. He made her feel cherished—loved.

For the first time she cried, and he held her gently with arms like steel, and cradled her against the safety of his chest.

Linsey found the restriction a mixed blessing. On the one hand, of course, she saw a lot more of Matthew and that had to be a plus. On the other hand she had no time on her own, no privacy, no personal space. For such an independent and undisciplined person, it was purgatory.

Only in her surgery hours was she alone, and then Matthew wanted to discuss the patients and go over her treatment plans and possible alternatives.

Her minor surgery, to her annoyance, he did anyway, and she was present and assisted if it was required. As there was also a nurse there she seldom was required, and her fingers itched to get on the end of the scalpel.

Then she had her chance. A young woman came in complaining of heavy, irregular periods of uncertain length, weight gain and headaches. She had been on the Pill for some years and had become pregnant by accident after forgetting to take it. After a termination she had had Norplant—a contraceptive implant consisting of tiny, soft, hollow rods, filled with a slow-release contraceptive, which were injected under the skin on the inside of the upper arm and provided cover for five years.

However, it didn't suit everybody, as was often the case with any hormone, and as a result she was having the side effects that had brought her to the surgery.

'I think the implant needs to be removed,' Linsey told her. 'I'm sorry, because of course it is very convenient, but there's no point making yourself ill.'

'No,' the girl agreed. 'I felt like this once with the Pill, but of course I just stopped taking that, and I've heard such a lot about these rods being difficult to remove.'

Linsey examined them and shook her head. 'I can feel them all quite easily, although they don't show. They should be easy to get out if they were put in right, and these do seem to have been. Who did it?'

'Dr Jarvis, but I was put on your list.'

She smiled. 'That's OK. We do our minor surgery together, so he'll probably do it anyway.'

'Oh,' the girl said, 'can't you do it?'

'I expect so. Why?'

The girl grinned. 'I just think you might be more gentle; not that he hurt me at all, but you being a woman. . .' She shrugged. 'It was just a thought.'

'I'll ask him. Can you come in tomorrow between eleven and eleven-thirty? Wear a T-shirt or something sleeveless so we can get at it easily. You'll have a local anaesthetic and then we'll make a little opening and lift the rods out one by one. There are six.'

'Yes, I know. That's fine. I'll be here.'

'And then, of course,' Linsey said, 'we need to decide what you're going to use next.'

'Could I have a coil?'

'An IUCD? Yes, I think so. I don't see why not. You need to be having a period to fit it—preferably a normal one, not a hormone-induced bleed like you've been having. Wait until you're back to normal and then ring up on the first day of your period and make an appointment.'

'And can you fit that?'

'Yes,' Linsey said definitely. Her obstetrics qualification covered her for contraceptive services, and under that umbrella she intended to take out the Norplant rods.

She discussed it with Matthew that evening while she was under what she was fast coming to think of as house arrest.

'They can be difficult to get hold of,' he warned. 'There's been a lot of hoo-ha in the Press.'

'But they're so easily palpable.'

'Of course—I put them in.'

She chucked a cushion at him. 'Matthew, I'm going crazy. I can't do this, I can't go there, I have to stay in—for God's sake!'

'All right,' he agreed mildly. 'Have a go. But I'll be there—'

'Hovering.'

He smiled innocently. 'I don't know what you mean.'

In the event she was quite glad to have him there, although she managed most of the rods without any trouble. One of them, though, was difficult and evasive, and although she was stubborn and opinionated she was also aware that this was her patient's arm and she had no business scarring it for life out of pique.

Matthew, to her annoyance, managed to locate and remove it with forceps on the second try, and she ground her teeth, smiled sweetly and thanked him.

'My pleasure,' he said, eyes dancing with appreciation of her self-control.

Later he mentioned it. 'Don't feel you failed because you couldn't get that one out. There's usually one that's a nuisance, and you managed the others well.'

'It's fiddly, isn't it?'

He nodded. 'I won't fit it any more. I think the idea was superb and the principle's a good one, but if there's a problem with side effects it's much harder to remedy than just stopping taking the Pill, and in any case it has to be removed after five years, so at some time you have to deal with the tricky business of extracting the rods. It's just another risk to add to the existing ones of oral contraception.'

'Talking of which, I'm thinking of coming off it. I'm getting fat.'

He put his arms round her and hugged her. 'You're gorgeous. You're not at all fat.'

'My clothes don't fit. Will you put me in an IUCD?'

'No.'

'Why?'

'Because they fail.'

'No, they don't.'

'They do. I mean it—I don't ever want children. I'd hate you to get pregnant by accident. It's bad enough knowing either of us could get hurt in our relationship, without introducing another innocent victim.'

'So we'll go back to condoms.'

He wrinkled his nose. 'I hate having anything between us.'

'You can't feel it.'

'But I can.'

She shrugged. 'Take your choice, then, because I'm coming off the Pill.'

He groused. 'Take another sort.'

'I don't like mucking about with nature,' she argued.

'Then I'll use condoms,' he agreed. 'I don't want you having a coil—or a baby.'

She felt a tiny pang, a sort of strange, almost biological regret in the region of her womb. Would he ever change his mind?

And would he ever admit he loved her? Possibly not.

'Isn't it time we had another tutorial?' she said. 'How about non-compliance with contraceptive advice?'

'Referral to the antenatal clinic, you mean?'

And he thought she was sarcastic!

Linsey decided she wanted to learn more about the endoscopy clinic, and so the next time they had a screening session she asked to be involved.

Rhys was running it, and he was screening three patients for peptic ulcers before treating them for *Helicobacter pylori*. The procedure, a simple one requiring the patient to relax and swallow a tube with a tiny camera on the end, usually involved sedation, but, Rhys explained, because it was being carried out in the little hospital at Milhaven and not in the bigger hospital at Lymington or the even bigger teaching hospitals at Southampton, and because it was being carried out by their own family doctor, the patients rarely needed more than a local anaesthetic spray in their throats.

'The infection has already been confirmed in these

people through a blood test, and under normal circumstances we'd simply give them eradication therapy for the *H. pylori* and then follow it up with a urea breath test to see if it was eradicated. Because these patients are over forty-five, though, we routinely screen them for malignancy.'

'Hence the gastroscopy.'

'That's right. Have you done any endoscopic work in the hospital?'

'A little,' she confirmed. 'I did tons of gastric washouts when I was in A and E, though, for overdoses.'

'Want to have a go?' he asked. They were scrubbing up for the first patient, and she was surprised he should offer her the opportunity.

'Why don't I watch the first one, and then do the second?' she suggested.

He chuckled. 'Where's your confidence? Matthew been getting at you again?'

She laughed. 'Matthew? I don't know what you mean!'

'So do the first.'

She looked at him seriously. 'You mean it, don't you?'

'Of course I mean it.'

She was touched. 'OK,' she agreed. 'I will—if the patient doesn't mind.'

The patient didn't, and, although he gagged a little on the tube at first, she was gentle and patient, Rhys held his hand and talked calmly to him, and the tube slipped easily down, giving them a clear view of the wall of his stomach. They watched the screen closely as she scanned the wall systematically until she finally found what she was looking for.

'Ouch. That looks nasty—I don't wonder you've been suffering,' Rhys said with a smile. 'Right, if we could have a little snippet of that for confirmation, Dr Wheeler?'

She snipped a tiny portion of the ulcerated area with the biopsy instrument contained in the gastroscope, and then checked further to make sure that there were no other ulcers lurking elsewhere.

There weren't, and so she gently and slowly withdrew the instrument. The patient coughed and sat up, swallowing hard and shaking his head.

'OK?' Rhys asked him.

'Yes, I suppose so. Not nearly as bad as I'd thought it would be.' His smile was wry. 'Thanks, Dr Wheeler.'

She flashed him a smile. 'My pleasure. I hope it wasn't too uncomfortable.'

'Not at all. You were very gentle. Thank you.'

Her smile widened. 'Just tell the other two on the way out, would you?'

He must have done, because once she and Rhys were ready and the instruments were sterilised and prepared the next patient came in, grinned and lay down. 'Piece of cake, he said,' the man told them.

Linsey grinned. 'Absolutely. Right, open your mouth for me and I'll spray your throat with local anaesthetic, so you don't feel any discomfort when the little tube goes down. . . Lovely, well done.'

He swallowed it without a murmur, and they were getting on famously until she spotted the site of the problem.

It was quite difficult to keep her face neutral. She had seen dissected stomach tumours before in anatomy classes, and during her time in surgery she had seen growths removed. Never had she seen one so large or so badly inflamed.

'Right, I think we've found it,' she said, looking to Rhys for confirmation.

He nodded, his face impassive. 'A small biopsy will confirm the diagnosis,' he said. 'It won't hurt.'

She snipped and withdrew the instrument, and, like the other man, the patient got up, smiled at them and left quite happily. Linsey looked at Rhys as the door swung shut behind him.

'Whoops,' she said softly.

'Somewhat,' he agreed. 'That's gone too far.'

'I thought so. What will you do?'

'Refer him immediately with the result. We'll treat him for *H. pylori* anyway, but the outcome is a foregone conclusion, I'm afraid. Oh, dear.'

'Do you know him?'

He shook his head. 'Not well. I treat his wife regularly—she's on HRT. She won't take it very well. I don't think she's very emotionally robust.' He shook his head and sighed. 'Ah, well, you win some, you lose some. Let's get cleaned up and hope the last one isn't bad news too.'

'While I think about it,' Linsey said as they scrubbed up again, 'how did Mr Joiner get on with the consultant? You remember, the guy with the CA prostate who had bone pain?'

'Ah. Yes, he had secondaries. It had metastasised to the spine and his hip. He's having radiotherapy to control the pain, but it's not a cure and he knows that. It might give him a little longer, though.

'Right, let's get this last patient seen and get back to the surgery.'

Linsey was an old hand by now. The procedure went without a hitch, they found a lovely innocent ulcer, took a biopsy and sent the man on his way.

'Funny that they're all men,' Linsey commented.

'It's just the way it works. We do screen women too whenever necessary. Right, let's get back and see what's new.'

Rhys had several calls to make, but Matthew had gone out to his own calls and Linsey's, to save her patients having to wait.

She went up to the flat and launched a bit of an assault on the mess, throwing their clothes in the washing machine and dumping the breakfast dishes in the sink. Having done that, she rang her aunt in Brighton and had a chat. The woman was alone now that her husband had died, and Linsey tried to provide some emotional support in the absence of any children.

'Interesting about that woman who came into your surgery and died,' her aunt said now. 'You know, the one with the label in her shirt.'

Woman? Linsey thought. Label? Casting her mind back, she remembered the very obese lady who had collapsed on the premises. 'Oh, that woman. Christine Cleary shirt.'

'That's the one! You know I knew her, did you? Sandra Jenkinson, her name was. We met in Christine's shop and had lunch together every now and again. Mind you, she was *dreadfully* overweight.'

This last said with studied emphasis. Linsey smiled. Her aunt was very far from slender. 'I'm glad recognising that label helped identify her. They might have been searching for weeks.'

'The strange thing was nobody bothered to report her missing. It's dreadfully sad that one could die and no one pays a blind bit of notice.'

Linsey actually thought it was probably the best way. She thought of Mr Joiner and his bone cancer, and the man she had seen today with his stomach tumour, and she wondered if it was indeed better to have loved and lost than never to have loved at all.

She thought how she would feel if Matthew died, and a stab of pain shot through her, so fierce that it took her breath away. And yet she was almost certain that he had no intention of letting their relationship drift into permanence. He didn't want children—he'd made that clear—and although she had found Rhys's little ones rather a handful that weekend, actually they had been sweet and quite fascinating in between the bad bits. She thought of never having any, and found the idea very sad.

She wanted Matthew's baby.

The realisation hit her like a freight train, and she actually had to sit down to let the shock pass. Lord, she really did want his baby. Was she actually putting on weight on the Pill, or was she simply considering coming off it because that would expose her to the risk of pregnancy?

After all, Matthew had got used to being able to make love to her anywhere, anytime, without thinking about contraception. It wouldn't take much to distract him.

Was that what was at the back of her mind?

Deception?

She decided to stay on the Pill.

CHAPTER NINE

THE grip of winter began to tighten on the Forest, and with it the grip of Linsey's frustration tightened on her.

It was dark now by four-thirty and so her curfew hours stretched endlessly. Rosie had retired, the receptionists were escorted home by Suzanne's husband, and the nurses drove home alone to their families.

Only Linsey was trapped, dependent on Matthew for every breath of air or step of exercise taken after dark.

There had been no further sign of the rapist, no more attacks, nothing. Linsey no longer felt as if she was being watched. She was never alone, and never threatened by anything except the incipient demise of her own sanity.

'I cannot stand it another minute!' she said to him one night as she paced the flat. 'It's absurd! Nothing is going to happen to me—nothing! We're stuck together all day and all night like Siamese twins—it's totally ridiculous.'

'You wouldn't say that if you'd been raped,' he said mildly, used to her rantings.

'But I haven't, and I won't be, because I never get a chance!' she raged.

'That's rather the idea,' he said pointedly.

'Don't patronise me!' she yelled. 'Matthew, I'm going mad! I want to be alone! I want to be able to make my own decisions, go where I want, do as I please. I cannot tolerate having my personal freedom dictated by this madman, and I won't put up with it!'

Matthew's mouth tightened. 'You can and you will. I simply won't allow——'

'Won't allow? Won't allow! What do you mean, you won't allow? Who the hell are you? What gives you the right to dictate to me?'

Go on, she thought, tell me you love me. Tell me you can't bear anything to happen to me because I mean more to you than life itself; tell me you can't stand the thought of another man touching me; tell me, damn it!

'You're right,' he said at last. He didn't look at her, just went into the bedroom and packed his things that were lying about.

'What are you doing?' she asked, cold dread filling her. Yes, she wanted her freedom, but not at the expense of Matthew's company.

'Going home,' he said flatly. 'I have no control over you, no sanctions, no rights. You're an independent woman. I'm sorry. I thought I was doing the right thing. I see now I was just being autocratic and high-handed. Of course you'll be sensible——but as your trainer and senior partner I can tell you that until further notice you will not be making house calls after dark, and I would be obliged if you would take over some other duties during the day to balance the books.'

Panic filled her. 'Matthew, don't be silly; I don't want you to go! Stay——talk to me.'

'There's nothing to say,' he told her. 'I'll see you in the morning.' He left without another word, leaving her stunned.

She went into the sitting room and looked out of the window at the car park below. He was getting into his car, throwing the things haphazardly into the back, slamming the door, reversing out in a spray of gravel and skidding out of the car park in a mass of wheel-spin and fish-tailing.

She watched his empty space until the security lights went out, and then plopped onto the nearest chair, eyes wide and sightless. Her chest felt as if a steel band was wrapped tightly round it, cutting off her breathing and squeezing her heart in a ruthless hand.

He was gone. She curled into the chair, knees under her chin, eyes staring blankly. What had she done? She had just been ranting, as usual—railing against her captivity. All right, he had been ridiculously over-protective, but she had never meant him to go. Not go, with all his things, for good.

As she sat there in the empty room a cold well of pain swamped her. 'Matthew,' she whispered. Her eyes closed, tears squeezed from beneath her lids, sliding down her cheeks and plopping wetly onto her knees. She couldn't let him go like this—she couldn't!

She wouldn't. She sat up, wiping her eyes against the sleeve of her sweatshirt. She would go after him and talk to him, reason with him, move in with him if necessary, if he wouldn't come back to her.

What if he wouldn't have her?

Doubts assailed her again, but she swallowed them and stood up. Car keys—she needed her car keys. And bag. Nothing else. She could change in the morning, if he let her stay.

She ran downstairs, set the alarm again for the practice and let herself out, locking the door securely behind her. It was raining, she realised—a cold, nasty drizzle that she hadn't expected—and she hadn't picked up a coat. Still, it was only a short distance to his house.

She started the car and pulled out, and as she turned up the road she saw a shadow move on the other side,

under the trees. Probably some hardy fool walking a
dog. She barely registered it.

The road was wet and nasty, and she shivered and
turned the heater up to maximum. It didn't make a lot
of difference at first, and by the time she turned onto
the road that led to Matthew's track her teeth were
chattering.

What had she been thinking of, coming out without
a coat?

Matthew, of course. Lord, if she'd lost him. . .

There were lights up ahead, and she slowed, puzzled.
A car was parked on the verge, slewed round at a strange
angle, and in the beam of its headlights she could see
something else—the underside of a car?

Dear God. There had been an accident. As she drew
level she saw that the car with its lights on was
Matthew's, and panic clawed at her throat. She stopped,
turning her car in so that she could see the upturned one,
and cut the engine, leaving the lights on and switching
on her hazard flashers with the last remnant of sane
thought.

Then she leapt out of the car and ran.

'Matthew? Matthew, where are you?'

'Here,' he called, his voice muffled. She could see
him now, lying beside the overturned car, his head in
through the window. He turned towards her. 'Linsey?
Get my bag from the car and come here. We've got two
casualties, both trapped.'

She got his bag as he said and ran over to him, slipping
and skidding on the wet leaves. 'Here.' She knelt down
and passed him the bag, almost delirious with relief at
finding he was all right.

'Thanks. My phone's in the car. I've rung the ambulance. Get them again and tell them to hurry, could you?

And then come back and give me a hand.'

'OK.' She ran back to the car and got the phone, then went back to him with it. 'What are the injuries?' she asked.

'I don't know. The driver's spitting teeth and bleeding copiously from various head wounds, the passenger's alive but barely—head at a strange angle, possible cervical fracture. Both are impossible to get at.'

She relayed that information, and was told that two ambulances with paramedics on board had been dispatched and the police were on their way. As she cut the connection she saw blue lights flash through the trees, and within moments an ambulanceman was running towards her.

'We need to get a line in to both of these people,' Matthew said to him. 'This one is semi-conscious; the passenger's out of it but potentially worse off. She needs a neck support before you do anything, but God knows how you'll get it on. And we need the fire brigade to lift the car off its roof so we can get at them.'

The ambulance driver made the necessary calls just as the police arrived.

She could hear the radios in the police car and ambulance burbling and crackling in the background, and lights were set up all round to give Matthew a better view.

Linsey passed him things—the giving set for the intravenous line, the bag of saline, the swabs to clear the mouth—

'Oh, my God, he's ripped his throat to pieces. The steering wheel's shattered and gone in his mouth and wrecked his palate. Possible fractured base of skull, and his mouth's swelling fast. I think I'll have to do a tracheotomy to give him an airway—that'll be jolly in these cramped surroundings.'

'I'll do it; my shoulders are smaller than yours—I can get in further,' Linsey said calmly. She didn't feel calm. The thought of climbing into that blood bath reeking of spilt petrol didn't fill her with joy and enthusiasm, but she didn't really think about it. It was her job, and she knew if she didn't get in there and do it the driver would die.

Matthew wriggled out backwards and she went in, dimly conscious of something sharp in her side. There was a light tucked under the upturned bonnet, illuminating the man's face and throat to perfection.

Not a pretty sight. She asked for the local anaesthetic, just in case he was conscious enough to feel the scalpel, but she didn't have time to give it to him. He started to gurgle, his ribs heaving helplessly, and she yelled, 'Now. I have to do it now!' The paramedic passed her a sterile pack containing a drape which she tucked round the man as well as she could, then she swiped a spirit swab over the site and quickly opened a hole in his windpipe. She found the tube in her hand, slid it in and was rewarded by the man's gasping breath.

She dropped her head onto her outstretched arm and let out a shuddering sigh.

'Done it?' Matthew asked, right behind her.

'Yes. He's OK now. I think we should get him out— if we can get the seat belt off. His feet don't seem to be trapped. It's only the passenger footwell that's collapsed.'

She wriggled out backwards, replaced by the paramedic carrying neck and back supports. After what seemed like an age he removed his head from the cabin and turned to them. 'I've supported his spine. Now we need to cut the belt and try and get him out, but he's looking a bit rough.'

'I'm not surprised,' Matthew said. 'It's an ancient car, no head restraints, sloppy fixed seat belts—a death trap.'

'Went fast enough to kill a pony,' the policeman behind them said drily.

Matthew nodded. 'I saw it there. Is it dead?'

'It is now—the vet's just been. Pregnant mare with a foal at foot. We've got the freeze-brand number and we're contacting the owner.'

'Damn, we've lost him—let's get him out,' the paramedic yelled, and, cutting the seat belt, he let the man slide to the roof of the car. Matthew grabbed one arm, the paramedic the other and, with Linsey supporting his head, they dragged the man out.

It was hopeless. Once he was out of the car the full extent of his head and chest injuries could be seen, and Linsey realised that nothing on earth could have saved him. She shuddered. What a horrible, gory end—and all because he had been driving too fast on a night as black as pitch and had hit yet another of the ponies, the innocent victims of the Forest. She looked round, and could see the foal standing some distance from its mother, nostrils flared because of the smell of blood, trying to make sense of the chaos and confusion.

'Poor little thing. It only looks a few months old.'

Matthew looked over his shoulder and grunted. 'It was lucky not to be hit too. What about the passenger?'

'Cervical fracture—probably third and fourth vertebrae,' the paramedic told him. 'I've got the collar on as well as I can. I think we're best to wait for the fire brigade before we try and get her out.'

Matthew nodded his agreement, then turned to Linsey. 'Why don't you go and wait at the house?'

She shook her head. 'I'll wait here,' she said, and shuddered violently.

He swore under his breath. 'Stupid woman, you haven't got a coat on! Here, put mine on and go and sit in the car.'

He ripped his coat off, pushed her arms down the wonderfully warm sleeves and buttoned it across her chest.

'What about you?' she protested feebly, snuggling into the cosy depths.

'I'll live. Go on.'

She stumbled up to her car, climbed behind the wheel and sat shivering while she watched the arrival of the fire brigade and the raising of the car. It was slow and laborious, but finally they raised it just enough to cut away the roof support and give Matthew and the paramedic room to ease the badly injured woman out. They had jacked open the footwell to free her, and she had broken legs, a crushed foot, almost certainly a broken neck and probably paraplegia.

Linsey wondered if they always did the right thing by saving lives. With the advent of technology and ever more powerful drugs, they seemed to have forgotten how to let people go.

She bent her head over the steering wheel and closed her eyes. She was still freezing, her hands and feet like ice, but at least she was shivering. That meant she hadn't managed to get too cold. In the icy drizzle it didn't take long to get hypothermia.

Her car door opened. 'Linsey? They're going now. We can go home.'

She lifted her head. 'Which home?' she asked him sadly. 'Yours, mine, or both?'

With a muttered oath he pulled her into his arms.

'What's the matter?' he said, and he sounded bitter. 'Miss me already?'

'Yes, as a matter of fact,' she mumbled into his shoulder.

He squeezed her and let her go. 'Come on,' he said. 'Let's go.'

His cottage was freezing. The heating was on tickover as he wasn't there much during the week, and he fiddled with the boiler, put the kettle on and led her into the sitting room.

'Sit here,' he said, and lit the gas stove that looked like a wood-burner. 'That's the advantage of gas,' he said with a forced smile. 'It warms up quicker than wood. Stay there; I'll get you a blanket and a hot drink.'

'I'm fine,' she protested.

'I'm not. I'm cold, I'm shocked and I'm covered in someone else's blood. Frankly all I want is a hot bath, and the second it's hot that's where we're going. Now shut up and stop being independent, and just let me look after you.'

She smiled. She didn't intend to argue with him. Not again. She snuggled down in the chair, her face angled towards the fire, and slept.

He woke her up a little while later. 'Bath's ready,' he told her.

She blinked and stretched, and stumbled after him up the stairs.

'Shower first,' he told her, and, stripping their clothes off, he pushed her under the pulsing spray of the shower. He washed her hair, just quickly, then his, and then cut off the water and dragged her across the now warm room to the bath.

'Get in.'

'Yessir,' she said smartly, and climbed in, sitting

down gingerly in the piping hot water. 'Oh, bliss.'

'Indeed.' He sat down with equal caution, turned on the bubbles and lay back with a sigh.

Their legs were tangled, hers between his, her toes tucked under his bottom. 'This is wonderfully decadent,' she mumbled sleepily, and wriggled her toes.

'All thanks to Joe. I would never have dreamed of being so self-indulgent, but I have to say there are times when it has its uses.'

She lifted her lids and looked at him. His gun-metal eyes were smoky-grey, smouldering with something primitive and possessive. She pulled her toes out from under his buttocks and walked them upwards, exploring his delicate masculine anatomy with curiosity.

He watched her, eyes hooded, and shifted one leg so that his toes could do a little exploring of their own.

Her eyes widened. How could he be so skilful with his toes? She laid the curve of her instep over the tempered steel of his response and slid her foot gently up and down.

He groaned and shifted, pulling her into his arms. 'Come here, witch. I need you,' he murmured, and without another word he drew her over him and guided her into position, then slid home with a sigh. 'Kiss me,' he ordered, and she bent forwards, her wet hair surrounding them, and took his mouth in a greedy, demanding kiss that escalated their loving from a mild and curious play to a blinding passion within seconds.

The bubbles stopped, but they didn't notice. Finally her skin grew cold and he eased her down beside him into the water, pressing the switch again.

The bubbles rose up, tickling them with warm air, easing out the stresses of the evening. He turned it on again twice more, then reluctantly helped her out of the bath and took her to bed.

'Is the surgery all secure?' he asked, and she nodded. He made no further reference to the fact that she was there with him and not at the surgery, but she couldn't just let it go so easily.

'Matthew, I'm sorry,' she said quietly, her hand resting on his chest. 'I didn't mean it to sound like it did. Of course I don't want to be raped, but I'm just feeling so restricted.'

'I understand. I'm sorry too. I'll try and give you more freedom, but it really is important at the moment to look after you. Just wait until he's caught.'

She thought of her confinement, then of the terrible aching sense of loss when Matthew had gone.

'OK,' she agreed. 'I'll wait.'

And then, she thought, I'll see if he still wants to be around. . .

Christmas was rushing up at twice the speed of light. For Rhys, who was struggling to cope with a demanding job and three even more demanding children, it meant a few blissful days off with his parents in Salisbury. He hadn't wanted to ask for the time, but Matthew had insisted.

Linsey wanted to stay with Matthew, and anyway, her parents were off on Boxing Day on a cruise, enjoying their early retirement. Tim was so wrapped up with April that they were more of a hazard than an asset, and so Matthew decided that he would cover Christmas Day and Boxing Day, sharing the daytime calls with Linsey. Where possible they would ask people to attend the surgery, and they would just hope everyone was so busy having a good time that they had some peace.

'We'll have two days off at the cottage afterwards,' he promised.

They were out of luck. The calls started in the wee small hours of Christmas morning, and went on without rest until ten.

Then, as Matthew pointed out cynically, everybody's guests were arriving and so they were too busy to disturb the doctor any more.

He refused to go to bed again but instead sat in a chair, a cup of coffee in his hand, and dozed off. Linsey removed the cup carefully and let him sleep. She had a present for him—a lovely, soft cashmere sweater that had cost half her salary but was so wonderful that she hadn't been able to resist it. It could wait until he was awake.

The phone rang and he mumbled something and cracked an eye open.

'I'll deal with it,' she told him firmly, and took the details. It was the neighbour of an elderly lady who had been feeling a little off colour. Could the doctor please come; the neighbour was going out for the day and was a bit worried about leaving her.

Linsey went out, enjoying the fresh air. It was a lovely day—bright and sunny although it was cold. Perhaps they'd take the mobile phone and go for a walk after Matthew woke up.

She found the elderly patient's house and parked outside, then rang the bell. She heard a feeble voice calling, then tried the door and found it open.

'Hello,' she called as she went in. 'It's Dr Wheeler.'

'Up here, dear,' the voice warbled. 'I'm in the front room.'

The house smelt of stale urine, Linsey noticed, and a pair of sticks stood at the bottom of the stairs. A quick glance in the kitchen showed that it was reasonably tidy but the gas ring looked ancient and dangerous, and she wondered how long the patient had been incontinent.

She ran upstairs and into the bedroom, and was nearly overwhelmed by the smell. 'Hello, there. Happy Christmas. I gather you're not feeling good.'

'Oh, I'm better now,' the old lady told her. 'Oh, I had such a bad day yesterday—I felt really off colour. Then in the night I had this sharp pain, right low down—you know, dear, *there*,' she explained in a raspy whisper. 'Oh, it did hurt. Then this morning I was lying on something and I found this.'

She produced a rough yellow object the thickness of a finger and about two inches long and handed it to Linsey. 'I can't imagine what it is,' she said bluntly, 'but I'm better off without it, I can tell you.'

Linsey stared at the object in amazement. 'Miss Lucas, it's a bladder stone,' she told her. 'You must have had it in there for ages.'

The woman blinked. 'Well, how did it get out?'

Linsey wasn't sure, short of a miracle. 'You must have passed it. Perhaps I'd better have a look at you and make sure you aren't torn.'

'What, down there?' She looked scandalised.

'Miss Lucas, it's all right; I'm a doctor,' Linsey said gently.

The elderly woman blushed. 'Well, if you have to. Oh, I never thought I'd have to go through anything like this.'

She submitted to the examination with profuse embarrassment, and Linsey was glad to get it over quickly. The smell in the bed was too awful to bear.

She looked around the bleak and empty room, and then back to the frail old lady in the bed. Was this going to be her Christmas? 'Are you doing anything today, Miss Lucas?' she asked her.

'No, dear. Nothing. Why?'

'Well, because if it wouldn't interfere with your plans I wondered if we wouldn't be better to let you spend a day or two in the cottage hospital, just to get over the experience. You'd have someone to cook your meals, and you'd be able to rest and get properly better.'

Her wrinkled, rheumy eyes brightened immediately. 'I wouldn't want to be a bother,' she said briskly, but Linsey could see that the idea had appeal.

'It's no bother, not for anybody. You'll get a nice Christmas lunch there today, as well.'

She definitely brightened at that. Linsey arranged for her admission, and while they waited for the ambulance she helped Miss Lucas find a few things and put them in a case. Then she went home and changed her clothes, throwing the smelly ones in the bin.

Matthew came out of the sitting room, sniffing. 'Have you wet yourself?'

'And Happy Christmas to you too. No, I've been with a patient. She passed this in the night.'

She handed Matthew the bladder stone which she had in her pocket.

'Good God. Is she split in half?'

Linsey chuckled. 'No, but she wasn't keen to let me look at her. She was amazingly unscathed. I gave her some antibiotics and I think she'll be fine.'

'Who was it?'

'Miss Lucas.'

'Really? She's as nutty as a fruit-cake. What did you do with her?'

She smiled. 'I admitted her to Milhaven. That way

she gets a bath, a Christmas lunch and the attentions of social services.'

Matthew kissed her. 'Clever girl. Talking of Christmas lunch, what time are we eating?'

She laughed. 'Your guess is as good as mine. I'll put the turkey in for six. When we eat is dependent on the vagaries of this crazy profession, I suppose.'

He slouched against the bedroom wall and watched her dress. 'We're having a turkey for the two of us?'

She grinned. 'Only a tiny one. I thought we ought to try and do it properly.'

He laughed and hugged her. 'I've got a present for you under the tree.'

'What tree?'

He grinned. 'I thought we ought to try and do it properly,' he mimicked.

She followed him into the sitting room and there in the corner was a little artificial tree, with a string of fairy lights and a few tiny ornaments. There was a present under it.

'Hang on,' she said, and went and fetched his from the bedroom, putting it with the other one. 'Do you suppose we could have a small sherry?'

He smiled. 'Probably a small one. Have you got any?'

'Of course. Why did you think I mentioned it? Just to wind us up?'

'It wouldn't be the first time. I can think of something else you often mention when I can't do anything about it.'

She smirked and rubbed up against him. 'I don't know what you mean.'

'Hussy. Get the sherry and come and open your present.'

She did, her fingers all thumbs as she tried to peel off the sticky tape.

'Just rip it before the phone rings again,' he growled impatiently.

'Well, you open yours— Oh, Matthew!'

The box lay open on her lap, the beautifully set semi-precious stones winking in the lights of the tree. With trembling fingers she lifted the necklace from the box and stared at it open-mouthed.

'Allow me,' Matthew murmured, and, taking the necklace from her, he placed it carefully round her neck. Then he led her to the mirror.

Each stone was simply but perfectly cut into a delicate oval, set within a fine gold band and linked together so that the ovals lay end to end in a softly glittering curve against her skin. There were moonstones, topazes and amethysts, pale emeralds and delicate zircons, the colours muted and exquisite.

'Oh, Matthew, you shouldn't. . .' she began, her eyes filling, and he shushed her and smiled.

'You look beautiful in it. I knew you would—you couldn't fail.'

She looked into the mirror again, her eyes misty. 'It's the most beautiful thing I've ever had in my life,' she said, choked, and turned into his arms and hugged him. Then she sniffed inelegantly and pulled away. 'Come on, you have to open yours. I'm afraid it's going to seem awfully tame.'

He pulled the wrapper off without any hesitation and lifted the jumper out with an exclamation of delight. 'Oh, Linsey, it's wonderful! So soft—where did you find it?'

She grinned. 'Salisbury last weekend, with Tricia. I

met her there—she was staying with her parents. Put it on.'

He tugged off the one he was wearing and pulled it carefully over his head.

She eyed him thoughtfully. 'It suits you.'

'It feels wonderful,' he said, straightening the bottom. 'Like cashmere.'

'It is.'

'Linsey!' His low reproach was belied by his eyes, warm with appreciation. 'Thank you.'

He pulled her into his arms and kissed her lingeringly.

Predictably, the phone rang.

'Again?' he groaned, and answered it.

It was like that for the rest of the day. By five forty-five they had had ten calls out and eight people to the surgery, and were wondering whether they would get their meal when the phone rang again.

'Don't they have anything better to do?' Matthew grumbled, and scooped it up. 'Jarvis,' he said briskly. 'Yes? What seems to be the problem? Right, OK. Where are you? Fine. I'll be with you in ten minutes.'

He put the phone down. 'Visitors in a holiday cottage. Elderly father has chest pain—I expect he's eaten too much Christmas dinner. Chance would be a fine thing. Go for dinner at six-thirty, OK?' He kissed her lingeringly, then, with a muttered sigh he dragged himself away and ran down the stairs.

Linsey watched him go with a soppy smile on her face. Her hand went up to her necklace again, feeling the warmth of the stones against her skin. Surely he must love her? she thought contentedly. Of course he did, just as she loved him. And tonight she'd tell him.

The phone rang again.

'Hello, Dr Wheeler speaking. Can I help you?'

It was a man's voice, hoarse and rasping. 'I'm sorry to disturb you,' he said. 'It's Mr Parker—I'm a patient of Dr Wilson's. I've got some kind of throat bug, a temperature, shivering. I wonder if I might pop round to the surgery? I'm only a few doors away.'

She eyed the kitchen. She had sprouts to cook, the gravy to make, the table to lay. . .

'Are you sure?' she asked him. 'It would be a help. We've been very busy.'

'Of course. Thank you.'

The phone went dead, and Linsey ran downstairs and switched off the alarm. She'd take him through into her consulting room, she thought. She put the lights on all through the surgery and waited, and a moment later the security lights outside switched on and the intercom buzzer went.

'Hello? Who is it, please?'

'Mr Parker,' the caller's voice rasped.

'Push the door and come in, Mr Parker,' she said, and went to greet him. 'Hello, there. Could you come into my consulting room and I'll have a look at you?'

She turned away and froze at the sudden, cold sound of sliding steel. A knife.

'I don't think so, Dr Wheeler. I think I'd like to go upstairs with you to your bedroom. I watch you getting ready for bed at night, you know. You're not always very sensible about closing the curtains, especially not when your boyfriend creeps up on you.'

Linsey swallowed, praying for inspiration. 'We can't go up there,' she lied. 'The alarm's on.'

'So unset it—and don't try any fancy stuff. This knife's sharp. I use it for filleting fish. If that alarm goes off, by the time help comes I'll be long gone—and your precious Dr Jarvis won't ever want to look at you again. . .'

CHAPTER TEN

LINSEY'S hands were shaking so badly that she could hardly press the numbers on the alarm keypad. Backwards, she told herself, then the alarm would sound only at the police station and Matthew's cottage. Not that that would help—he wasn't there—but at least the police would come—if she got it right.

Nothing. No alarm. Thank God. The keypad display light went out, showing the system open. Please, God, let it work, she prayed.

'Right,' the harsh, ugly voice said behind her. 'Let's go. I want my Christmas present, Dr Wheeler. I've waited a long time, but you've made it more interesting. I thought he'd never leave you alone, but he did. I knew it was just a matter of patience.'

Linsey went slowly up the stairs, her heart pounding. Please, Matthew, come back. Please let the alarm work. Please hurry, police—

'Faster, Dr Wheeler. I'm getting impatient.'

She felt the prick of the knife against her thigh, and ran up the last few steps, the madman right behind her.

'Now, into the bedroom, nice and easy, without turning on the light—lovely. Shut the curtains. I'd hate anyone to see this. This is for me. Just me.'

He flicked the light on, and then tossed her something white—a T-shirt? She caught it automatically and stared at it.

'Put it on,' he ordered. 'Take everything off and put it on.'

176

She looked at him in horror. 'My nightshirt—how did you get this?'

He laughed—an ugly sound. 'I slipped in behind your not so vigilant lover one night, but before you came back to me a burglar disturbed me. I thought it prudent to make myself scarce, but I took it with me as a memento—something with your scent on to sleep with at night, and to remind me of you. Not that I've forgotten you, not for a minute. The last girl was just a distraction. Her hair was similar, you know, but not as beautiful as yours. Once I'd seen yours I realised the first girl was just a pale shadow too. It was you I really wanted all along. You should be flattered.'

She swallowed. Flattered? she thought. Try terrified. Where were the police? How could it take them so long? She'd have to waste time, distract him or something.

She took off her shoes, one by one, then fumbled with the hem of her jumper. Oh, God, she couldn't bear his eyes on her but she had to do something so that he would think she was co-operating—

'Come on!' he snarled. 'Now. I've waited long enough.'

She closed her eyes, grasped the hem of her jumper again and prayed.

Matthew couldn't find the cottage. He was sure the man had said it was down this road, but there was no trace of anything answering its description.

He drove to his cottage, meaning to phone Linsey and ask her to contact him if the man rang back, and as he got out of the car to open the gate he heard it.

Not the shrill wail of his house alarm, but the insistent beep-beep-beep of the surgery-alarm system connected to his house.

The blood drained from his face. A hoax, he thought—a hoax to get him away from the surgery, leaving Linsey alone.

'Oh, God, no,' he whispered, and, throwing the car into reverse, he shot backwards down the track, out into the lane and then forward towards Milhaven, tyres screaming, the automatic gearbox protesting at the harsh treatment.

He put his headlights on full, fumbled the magnetic flashing green light out of the glove box and plugged it into the cigar lighter, then opened the window and stuck it on the roof, all with one hand. The car swayed and steadied, and he screamed down the road at twice the legal limit, praying that nothing got in his way.

He had to get to her. Nothing else mattered. She might only have one chance.

As he turned into the high street a police car shot past him, siren wailing, and turned up the practice road. He followed it, skidding into the car park and hitting the gravel at a run.

Hands trembling, he unlocked the back door and flung it open. 'Linsey? Where are you?' he shouted, terror clawing at him.

'Up here,' Linsey called, and he ran four steps at a time up the double flight, the policeman hard on his heels.

He almost fell over them.

A man was lying face down on the landing floor, white with pain, and Linsey was sitting on him, holding his arm at an unnatural angle behind his back. In the background Matthew was aware of another insistent beep, like the alarm at his cottage.

He reached for Linsey. 'Are you all right?' he asked her, lifting her up as the policeman took over, handcuffing the man's hands behind his back.

He screamed.

'Be careful. I might have broken his arm,' Linsey said in a curiously flat voice, and turned to Matthew. 'Could you turn the oven off? I think the turkey's cooked.'

'Are you really all right?'

She dredged up a small smile. 'I will be. I thought he was going to fillet me with that knife.'

A shudder ran through her and Matthew's face hardened. 'I could kill him,' he said softly.

Linsey smiled wryly. 'I nearly did. I was so tempted. The knife was just there, but I thought, What will it achieve? Nothing.'

'So you broke his arm instead.'

'That was an accident. I only had one chance. The oven-timer went off and he spun round, thinking it was the alarm. I jumped him and yanked his arm up—rather too hard, I'm afraid.'

'Don't be,' Matthew growled. 'It's giving me great satisfaction to know he's in pain.'

'That's terrible,' she reproached him.

'So it might be. It's how I feel. When I think what he could have done to you—'

He broke off, his jaw working, and Linsey felt her eyes fill. 'Matthew?'

'Mmm?'

'Hold me?'

He stood up and came over to where she was lying on the sofa. 'Are you sure? I didn't want to crowd you after—you know.' His shoulders lifted a fraction, his eyes creased with concern.

'I've told you before—you never crowd me. Please—just hold me. I need you.'

He perched beside her on the edge of the sofa, his arms coming carefully round her and lifting her against his chest as tenderly as they would an injured child. 'Oh, God, Linsey, I thought I'd be too late,' he said unsteadily, and, burying his face in her hair, he dragged in a shuddering breath.

Her arms slid round him, clinging to him, and finally she felt safe enough to let the healing tears fall. When she finally hiccuped to a halt Matthew lifted his head and gave her a ragged smile, and she saw that his cheeks were wet.

'Don't tell me you care,' she teased, her voice uneven, and he tipped his head back and fought for control.

'Oh, God, Linsey, if you only knew how much. . .'

She laid her hand on his shoulder. 'I wish I did,' she said softly. 'I wish you'd tell me. I've loved you so much for so long, I don't think I can bear it any more if you don't love me.'

He stared at her in amazement. 'Not love you? Of course I love you. I thought you found me such a pain.'

Her brow creased. 'A pain?' she said, puzzled. 'Why?'

'Always there, following you round, trapping you—'

'It was that lunatic that was the pain, not you. I never wanted to get away from you.'

His breath came out in a shaky whoosh. 'I thought you were bored with me.'

She laughed in surprise. 'Bored? How could I be bored?'

'Easily. I'm not exactly the world's most exciting person.'

Her face fell. 'Is that what you think? That I'm expecting you to entertain me? Matthew, I love you. I don't care about being entertained. I just need to know you're there for me—' She broke off, tears welling in her eyes. 'I need you with me. I'm nothing without you.'

'That's nonsense. You're beautiful and vivacious and intelligent and kind and funny and gifted medically— you're wonderful. What the hell do you see in me?'

She smiled mistily. 'Your eyes. I used to dream about your eyes. I was obsessed by you, did you know that? I had to close my eyes if anybody kissed me because their eyes were the wrong colour.'

'You're in love with my eye colour?' he said hollowly.

She laughed and pulled him down against her. 'Amongst other things. You're quite a nice person, really, when you try, and you've got a wonderful voice, and you're super with patients, and you've got the most interesting bathroom I've ever been in— Oh, and I forgot—you don't have genital warts.'

His face was a picture. 'Damn it,' he began, and then he laughed, hugging her up against his chest and nearly cracking her ribs. 'You have no respect at all. And none of those are good reasons.'

She could hear the hesitation in his voice, the uncertainty. She smiled and threaded her fingers through his hair, cradling his head against hers. 'Did I tell you what a wonderful lover you are? How generous and thoughtful? Or that I know you'll never let me down, and you'll always be there for me, putting me first, no matter how inconvenient? Did I mention how for the first time in my life someone has actually cherished me and made me feel fragile and precious instead of huge and ungainly?'

'You aren't huge and ungainly!' he protested, lifting his head away and peering down at her.

'I've always felt it before. And loud and clumsy.'

His grin was slow but worth waiting for. 'You can be clumsy sometimes,' he admitted. 'Just a tad. And you don't ever give up.'

'Oh, no. Not if I want something.'

His face became serious. 'And do you want me? I mean really want me, warts and all, for the rest of my life?'

'Oh, Matthew, you know I do,' she whispered.

'No, I don't. I know you want me now, but I don't know that you always will. No one else ever has. They've all got bored, like Judy got bored with Rhys—'

'Please don't compare me with Judy,' she said flatly. 'I'm nothing like her, and if you think I could ever do that to you then there's no point in us going on. I'm a one-man woman, Matthew—and you're that man. I haven't wanted anyone else since I first saw you. You looked at me, and I swear I could have walked across the water to you.'

He laughed awkwardly. 'You were drunk.'

'I'd been drinking,' she corrected him. 'Not that much. I knew you were special, even then.'

'I used to fantasise about you,' he told her, 'and you were beautiful and meek and submissive—'

She laughed helplessly. 'Me? Submissive?'

His grin was wry. 'You can see why you were such a shock to me. The real fantasy was a bit stronger than the pale imaginings of my youth.'

'I should hope so. Submissive?' She chuckled. 'I should think not. I hope you're not expecting me to be a subservient wife, are you?' she added, and then could have bitten her tongue. Had he mentioned marriage? No, she didn't think so. Oh, Lord, what if he hadn't meant that?

'Good God, no,' he said in horror. 'I'm expecting you to be a thoroughly aggravating and difficult wife. You'll challenge every decision I try and make, question my judgement on every issue and generally interfere with the smooth running of our matrimonial home at every turn. What else could you do? You wouldn't be you if you didn't.'

She snuggled closer. 'Just so long as you realise what you're getting.'

'Oh, I realise,' he murmured. 'And I can't tell you how much I'm looking forward to it.'

His lips brushed hers, just gently. Too gently. He was being careful and considerate, she realised, not knowing what the rapist had done to her.

'He didn't touch me,' she said quietly.

Matthew went still. 'What?'

'The rapist. He didn't touch me. You don't have to be careful. I'd rather you weren't. I'd like you to drive me out of my mind with need for you so I forget all about it.'

'Are you sure?' he asked gently.

'Quite sure. Make love to me, Matthew—please?'

He needed no second bidding. He scooped her up in his arms, carried her into the bedroom and slowly and methodically drove her out of her mind.

For once she didn't interfere or take charge or question what he was doing; she just lay there, eyes fixed on him as she spiralled higher and higher. He took her to the brink again and again, and then finally went over the edge with her.

Then he laid his cheek against hers and their tears mingled on the pillow. . .

'You'll forgive me for not being there, won't you?' Rhys said gently. 'It's just that weddings and I don't get on at the moment.'

Linsey kissed his cheek. 'We understand. Please don't

feel bad about it. And thank you so much for your present.'

He smiled—a little quirk to a mouth that smiled too rarely. 'My pleasure. Just enjoy yourselves.'

He had given them the weekend—paid for the honeymoon suite and all meals in a lovely hotel in the New Forest. It was unbelievably generous, and to make it possible he was covering the practice from Saturday morning to Monday morning. Tim was doing Friday night, because, as he said candidly, it was no good if the groom was going to be too tired to be any use.

The wedding was very simple. Tricia was there, staying with her parents in Salisbury and delighted to meet Matthew at last.

'Keep her in line, please. I've spent two years training her to be tidy; don't let her throw it all away.'

'How could something so tiny have such a dominating influence over you?' he said to Linsey later over dinner, courtesy of Rhys.

Linsey laughed. 'Only her body's tiny. Her determination is enormous. You think I'm bad? If she wants something, she gets it.'

Matthew reached over, picked up her hand and twiddled her wedding ring. 'I haven't noticed you exactly failing to get what you want.'

She smiled lazily. 'Darling, I've hardly started.'

His eyes widened. 'Oh, God. Why did that sound like a threat?'

She laughed—a throaty, feminine laugh that made his body clench. 'Relax. You'll love every minute of it.'

Matthew wasn't at all sure he liked the sound of that. . .

EPILOGUE

LINSEY lay sprawled across the bed, her body slaked. Her mind, however, was restless. There was something she and Matthew had to talk about.

She turned on her side and faced him, running a finger gently over his chest and down to his tummy-button. Idly she picked the fluff out of it. 'Matthew?'

'Mmm?'

'You forgot again.'

He cracked one eye open, his brow furrowed for a moment, then he dropped his head back and sighed. 'Damn. Sorry.'

'That's the second time this week. You're getting careless.'

He opened his eyes again and turned towards her. 'I am? What about you? You could have reminded me.'

'You made me forget my own name. I was past caring about birth control.'

He smiled—a feral smile of great masculine satisfaction. 'That good, eh?'

She punched his shoulder. 'You know it was. It always is. Don't change the subject.'

'What is the subject?' he asked softly.

She looked down, away from those eyes that understood her all too well. 'Are you doing it on purpose?'

'Forgetting? No.'

She ran her hand over his chest. 'I just wondered.'

'Wondered what?'

She shrugged. 'If you'd changed your mind.'

He lifted her chin so that she had to meet his eyes. 'About what?'

'Babies,' she said flatly.

He searched her eyes. 'Do you want a baby?'

She swallowed. 'Only if you do. I wouldn't want to do anything you didn't want—'

His laugh cut her off. 'That's priceless,' he said when he could speak. 'You manipulate me, engineer my life, boss me about—you make Mussolini look like a regular sweetheart, and then you tell me you don't want to do anything I don't want to do? Since when?'

She scooted up the bed and folded her arms. 'Not about such a major issue,' she said grumpily. Heavens, was she really that manipulative?

He reached up and rolled her down against him, cradling her head against his chest. 'Darling, if you want a baby, we'll have a baby.'

'But eighteen months ago you wanted a vasectomy.'

He chuckled. 'Only fleetingly. Three kids were a bit much all at once. One at a time I could probably cope with. Besides—' he ran his hand up her thigh, absently caressing the soft curve of her tummy '—the caveman in me quite fancies the idea of you swollen with my child.'

She sighed with relief. 'I'm glad about that,' she said quietly, 'because the first one's due in eight months.'

He went very still then shifted his head and peered at her. 'It is?'

She watched, breathlessly as the smile lit his eyes. 'Oh, darling. . .' His hug was bone-cracking, but she didn't care. She had one more thing to ask.

'About my maternity leave.'

He shifted and looked at her again. 'Yes?'

'Can Tricia do it?'

His eyes widened. 'Tricia? The demon Tricia?'

She giggled and punched him. 'You like her.'

'I do?' he said in astonishment. 'She's worse than you.'

'Mmm. You'll feel you got a bargain in me if she's around.'

He hugged her. 'I did get a bargain—and yes, Tricia can do your maternity leave if she wants so—just until we get another doctor to take over from you.'

'I don't want to give up work, Matthew.'

'No.'

'Matthew? Matthew, don't ignore me!'

'I wouldn't dare,' he said drily. 'I wouldn't dare. . .'

In THE IDEAL CHOICE
Rhys meets his match in Tricia.
Watch next month for their
enthralling romance.

GET 4 BOOKS
AND A MYSTERY GIFT

Return this coupon and we'll send you 4 Mills & Boon Medical Romance™ novels and a mystery gift absolutely FREE! We'll even pay the postage and packing for you.

We're making you this offer to introduce you to the benefits of Reader Service: FREE home delivery of brand-new Mills & Boon Medical Romance novels, at least a month before they are available in the shops, FREE gifts and a monthly Newsletter packed with information.

Accepting these FREE books and gift places you under no obligation to buy, you may cancel at any time, even after receiving just your free shipment. Simply complete the coupon below and send it to:

MILLS & BOON® READER SERVICE, FREEPOST, CROYDON, SURREY, CR9 3WZ.

No stamp needed

Yes, please send me 4 free Mills & Boon Medical Romance novels and a mystery gift. I understand that unless you hear from me, I will receive 4 superb new titles every month for just £2.10* each postage and packing free. I am under no obligation to purchase any books and I may cancel or suspend my subscription at any time, but the free books and gifts will be mine to keep in any case. (I am over 18 years of age)

M6JE

Ms/Mrs/Miss/Mr _____

Address _____

_____

_____ Postcode_____

mps MAILING PREFERENCE SERVICE

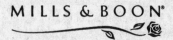

MILLS & BOON®

Medical Romance™

Books for enjoyment this month...

THE REAL FANTASY	Caroline Anderson
A LOVING PARTNERSHIP	Jenny Bryant
FOR NOW, FOR ALWAYS	Josie Metcalfe
TAKING IT ALL	Sharon Kendrick

Treats in store!

Watch next month for these absorbing stories...

THE IDEAL CHOICE	Caroline Anderson
A SURGEON'S CARE	Lucy Clark
THE HEALING TOUCH	Rebecca Lang
MORE THAN SKIN-DEEP	Margaret O'Neill